COD
STREUTH

C O D
STREUTH

Bamber Gascoigne

JONATHAN CAPE
THIRTY-TWO BEDFORD SQUARE
LONDON

First published 1986
Copyright © 1986 by Bamber Gascoigne
Jonathan Cape Ltd, 32 Bedford Square, London WC1B 3EL

British Library Cataloguing in Publication Data
Gascoigne, Bamber
Cod streuth.
I. Title
823'.914[F]   PR6057.A724
ISBN 0-224-02388-8

Typeset by Computape (Pickering) Ltd, Pickering, North Yorkshire
Printed in Great Britain by
Butler & Tanner Ltd, Frome and London

CONTENTS

INTRODUCTION

T HERE ARE NOT MANY readers of the *Journal* of the
Historical Society of São João del Rei (founded with high
and solemn aims in 1864 but defunct by 1870), which would
explain why the set in the British Library still had its
yellowing pages uncut more than a century later. And why
the extraordinary story of Jacques le Balleur remains apparently unknown.

The volume for 1868 came to me by a happy accident. I had
applied for the *Annual Proceedings* for that year of the Birmingham Society of Chromolithographers and Allied Crafts. The
shelf mark of this publication is *Ac. 2436.* When the volume
arrived, its exterior revealed at once that there was a mistake.
The uneven deckle edges to the pages, a dust-collecting
custom which survived longest in Roman Catholic countries,
did not suggest Birmingham in the 1860s. The spine proved
that the fault was mine, in a too hastily written '3', for this
volume was *Ac. 2476.*

The title page was virginal, intact on two sides and as yet
unsullied by the eye of a reader, so it was impossible to tell
what chance had delivered. But the book fell open at the end of
the first section, and I saw that it was in Portuguese.

Three adjacent words at the top of the recto seemed to leap
off the page. *Calvinistas e canibais.* A link between Calvinists
and cannibals was too intriguing to ignore. I called for a paper
knife.

The ravished title page revealed that this was the fifth issue
of the *Journal* of a learned institution which gratefully bene-
fited to an inexpressible degree from the patronage of the very

7

holy Archbishop of São Sebastião do Rio de Janeiro and of the egregious Monsignor Miguel Coimbra, Dean of the Confraria Episcopal de São Francisco e São Gonçalo, this year's offering being the previously unpublished *Monthly Reports of Evil Intent and Practice by the Recidivist Jacques le Balleur in the Years Following 1560*, edited by Luis Agostinho da Caminha, Librarian of the Public Library and Secretary of the said Society.

The librarian, fortunately for us, was an idle editor. He seems to have considered the historical part of his task complete when he had penned his extraordinary Preface. Beyond that, Senhor da Caminha limited himself to translating the French text from the dried bundle of leaves which had fallen into his hands. Clearly the academic standards of São João del Rei were not exacting. The advantage of this is that the material remains, in effect, untampered with.

I too have preferred to let Jacques speak for himself, perhaps because I have as much sympathy for him as the librarian had scorn, but I have added brief comments where clarification seemed necessary. As is conventional, all editorial additions are in square brackets.

One cannot blame da Caminha for not pointing out the importance (in terms of South American studies) of the sexual kingship encountered by Jacques in the highlands of Brazil, for at that time this custom had not yet been described in *The Golden Bough* in its better known African form. A more reprehensible omission on the part of my predecessor was his failure to print the ten pages of Rabelais which became the 'bible' of one remote Brazilian tribe for a few years in the sixteenth century. The reason was presumably that there was no copy of the French text in his library, but it must have made the story hard to follow for the members of the Historical Society. From the edition which Jacques had with him (Troyes, 1556) it becomes quite clear which ten pages survived in his pocket until the moment when he was dis-covered by the Tupinilis. I have included them as an Appen-dix. All quotations from Rabelais in the text are printed in italic.

My other main contribution has been the dating of the separate entries in the *Monthly Reports*. This would have been difficult for Senhor da Caminha without modern works of scholarship, for it involved discovering the date of the comet which preceded the death of Jacques and then working back through some forty new moons in the 1560s.

The tone of da Caminha's Preface, which I print without alteration, is in keeping with the mood among Roman Catho-lics at that time (the pontificate of Pius IX), but was no doubt characteristic also of the man himself, of whom we have just one tantalising glimpse.

Richard Burton, restless traveller in South America as well as India, Arabia and Africa, was briefly in São João del Rei during the summer of 1867, the year before the publication of the *Monthly Reports*. He was shown round the town by Mr Charles C. Copsy, of Cambridge, who had found employ-ment there as Lieutenant-Colonel of seventy-four Brazilian volunteers and as Professor of English, Geography and Mathematics at the Lyceo. He guided Burton first to the Municipal Palace, housing the magistrates' court and the gaol. Burton continues:

> To the north is the Public Library, open every day and grimly decorated with the portrait of a local benefactor. The present librarian is stone deaf, and ignores the number of volumes under his charge. We guessed 3,200, and were corrected by the 'Almanak', which says upwards of 4,000.

Idle, stone deaf and ignoring the volumes under his charge — the words are not mine but they do seem irresistibly apt for my predecessor who, that very summer, must have been polishing his Preface while he awaited impatiently the comments of Monsieur Lebel in Rio de Janeiro on the accuracy of his translation.

PREFACE

by
Luis Agostinho da Caminha
Librarian of the Public Library

Through the study of history God speaks obliquely to His creation. If we are to learn from the recorded failings of others like ourselves, the virtues He will require of us are a cool head when confronted with the more lurid aspects of vice and corruption, and a clear eye for the links between then and now, between them and us, between the errors of the dead and the temptations which confront the living. The moral to be drawn, that is the true prize for the historian. It was an historian's insight that St Irenaeus displayed when he demonstrated how the evil done to mankind through the wickedness of Eve, mother of man, was annulled in the virtue of Mary, mother of God, proving through her Son that though the tempter snake be always with us, the victory shall not necessarily be his.

In most cases the historian is concerned with elucidating those events which demanded the attention of the people alive at the time. These will be amply recorded in contemporary documents. Thus we know of Martin Luther or Jean Calvin through countless contemporary tracts. It is the task of the responsible historian to sift this familiar evidence, with unblinking eye and none too

11

fastidious nostrils, so as to reveal in a balanced and objective manner the harm done to mankind by these venomous renegades from the loving embrace of the Church.

But sometimes God brings to the historian's notice some startling example of man's persistent folly which has remained until now undiscovered, unrevealed, unlearnt from. The perusal of such a document is the highest privilege of our profession, and its publication is an event of unusual importance in the annals even of a Society such as ours.

To be so singled out by Providence is an honour not given to every historian, but such was destined to be my good fortune when, on 3 July 1864, I opened the cupboard below the stairs leading up from the assistant librarian's desk to the storeroom below the clock in the Public Library of São João del Rei. I was accompanied by Senhor José Lopes, the caretaker, it being part of my duty, as Librarian, to pronounce judgement in a balanced and objective manner on a complaint by Senhor Lopes that there was insufficient room in the cupboard for his brooms. He pointed out that the cupboard was by long tradition known as the broom cupboard, but he maintained that by a process of creeping intrusion the 'rubbish' (his word) of the assistant librarian was steadily crowding out his brooms. Senhor Fernando Pereira, the assistant librarian, countered with the argument that the point at which the cupboard ceiling, descending beneath the stairs towards the floor, became too low to accommodate an upright broom had always been accepted as the beginning of the space where any material unclassifiable by normal cataloguing criteria (cataloguing being the assistant librarian's special responsibility) could be stored until further notice. Having myself joined the Library as its senior officer, rather than climbing through its ranks, the cupboard had been no concern of mine and I entered it now for the first time.

There was indeed evidence of contention between Senhor Lopes's brooms and Senhor Pereira's boxes, the two seeming at certain points almost inextricably inter-connected. The need for the brooms was self-evident, and my first thought therefore was to enquire whether a similar level of necessity attached to the contents of the boxes. I lifted one, large but surprisingly light, and passed it out to the assistant librarian.

'What, for example, is that?' I asked.

A very faded label, in a hand which my historian's eye judged at a glance to date from the eighteenth century, stated: 'From Mother Teresa, Superior of the Convent of São Felipe, Barbacena.' Senhor Pereira said that he knew nothing about the box, having been only seventeen years at his post and the degree of disorder which he had inherited from his predecessor having proved almost beyond even his powers of amendment.

I instructed Senhor Pereira to open the box. If there was a hint of unspoken rebuke in my tone, I now without qualification apologise. For I was soon to be profoundly grateful that neither Senhor Pereira nor anyone else of his limited professional abilities had attempted to classify or dispose of this valuable material.

The content of the box was not leaves, in the sense in which a Librarian normally uses the term, but actual *leaves* – large, brown, wrinkled, pierced through the centre on a long pointed rod similar to an arrow, and bringing to mind more than anything else a bundle of tobacco as hawked through the streets even today in the poorer districts of this town.

On both sides of each leaf there was writing, as wrinkled and shrivelled as the leaves themselves but still just legible. A note inside the lid revealed that a native had brought the contents of the box to the convent gate in Barbacena in 1765 (my estimate of the date of the handwriting thus being proved correct) and that the Mother Superior had paid him the price he asked when she saw the opening words on the first leaf: 'O Lord and Saviour Jesus Christ, Only Begotten and Beloved Son of Almighty God.' Later she had inspected the document more closely and had decided that this was not suitable material to be housed in a convent. The Mother Superior therefore packed up the leaves and sent them to the nearest library with archive facilities. Here they have remained ever since.

The deciphering, transcribing and translating of this material has been my constant labour during much of the past four years, and I freely confess that at times it was only my lifelong devotion to Clio which prevented my turning aside from an increasingly distasteful task. I found myself, as members of the Society will discover, in shameful company indeed – that of Calvinists and cannibals. But if we take the precaution of equipping ourselves with the proverbial long spoon, supper with the devil is almost invariably instructive. And so it is that I have immersed myself for history's sake in a tale of unbridled debauchery, lust, greed, duplicity, indeed almost every darkest aspect of our carnal nature, spiced

with the sickly sauce of pseudo-philosophy and sup-
posedly pious intentions.

Here, for all to see, is the naked form of that heresy
which assumed respectability in the sober bonnets of
Geneva and the well-cut habits of Port Royal. Here is
proof of what will occur if sinful man presumes to follow
his own conscience without the guiding hand of the
Church's authority. Here, with a writhing of naked limbs
and a stench of burning flesh reminiscent of the visions
recorded by the immortal Tuscan, is the Hell that man has
carried within himself ever since Adam first listened to
the soft voice of Eve. Here is recorded, step by step, the
degradation of Jacques le Balleur, apostate monk, student
of the pernicious schoolmaster Calvin at Geneva, mer-
cenary with the invading force of Frenchmen who from
1556 to 1560 forcibly occupied an island in the bay of
Rio de Janeiro, and finally heretic colonist somewhere
in the inaccessible highlands of our beloved Brazil.

Forming in himself a previously unknown corner of
history, Jacques le Balleur is perforce the sole witness to
his own degradation. His *Monthly Reports* constitute
what we historians call a primary source. They reach the
present readers in an unusually trustworthy state,
without the distortions so often imposed by earlier
editors, untrained in their exacting craft. The text
follows the sequence of leaves as they were spiked on
their rod. No leaf has been omitted.

It is usual on these occasions to offer profuse and
heartfelt thanks to any colleague who may have assisted
in the great task. Would that I could do so. Unfortunately
Monsieur Jean Lebel, *attaché* at the French embassy
in Rio de Janeiro, is entirely responsible for this volume

appearing a year later than it was originally promised to members of the Society.

Though my own French has on occasion been described by natives of that country as rather more than passable, I felt that I should solicit a second opinion on the accuracy of my translation in view of the increased difficulty inherent in a sixteenth-century original. I therefore sent to the French embassy a copy of my transcript of the text together with my version in Portuguese. Three letters and the passage of nine months at last elicited from the embassy, in the person of Monsieur Lebel, several pages of emendations. In many cases the proposed Portuguese alternatives seemed eccentric, to express the matter in the mildest possible form, and in places the pagination did not even tally. Two more letters, marked Express and Urgent, failed to provoke any response. The printer's deadline approached, after which another whole year would be missed, and I finally took the decision, without great enthusiasm, to allow a native Francophone to be my authority in this matter.

Those of Monsieur Lebel's emendations have been inserted, therefore, for which the proper context could be identified. I am tempted to reverse the normal convention and to conclude by saying that while any felicities of translation remain my own, unfortunate errors should in all probability be laid to the charge of Monsieur Lebel.

L.A.d.C.
S.J.d.R.
A.D.1868

[Senhor da Caminha's 'acknowledgement' must surely be unique in the annals of Academe, and I am happy to say that I can with a good conscience follow the more normal course. I have been greatly assisted by Dr Mario da Silva of the Portuguese embassy in London, who has very thoroughly checked my English version against da Caminha's Portuguese. He confirms my hunch that the Portuguese is in a standard nineteenth-century idiom, with no attempt at reproducing the tone of Jacques le Balleur's sixteenth-century original. It therefore seemed pointless to give a period flavour to my own version, though the robust quality of English prose at that time was richly tempting and would have given an appropriately lusty veneer to some of Jacques's experiences. However, in so far as one can judge through the filter of Luis Agostinho da Caminha, Jacques seems to have written about even his bawdy adventures more in the manner of Montaigne than of Rabelais, so the relative discretion of polite modern English may not be inappropriate.

I have made an exception only in the matter of quotations from Rabelais, for in this case we have a much-loved English version, more Rabelaisian than Rabelais himself, which appeared only a century after the experiences recorded by Jacques le Balleur. The famous translation by Sir Thomas Urquhart was published from 1653 onwards. Urquhart had been born in 1611, the very year of the King James version of the Bible. His language is therefore in the tradition which older English readers will always think of as appropriate to holy writ, and for that reason too I decided against a modern translation of Rabelais. The relevant section from Urquhart is given on pages 172–80.

I also have to thank Senhor Pedro Chagas, the present librarian in São João del Rei. To my enquiry whether there was any trace of the original tobacco leaves (for the text makes plain that this is what they were), with a suggestion that the broom cupboard under the stairs below the clock be thoroughly searched, I received a very prompt reply to the effect that the old library had been pulled down and a new one built on the site in 1956.

Senhor Chagas had been unaware of the article in the *Journal* for 1868 and naturally was eager to discover such a significant sixteenth-century document somewhere in his collection. The catalogue yielded no clues. Senhor Chagas did, however, unearth all the documents relating to the clearance of the old building. The contents of the cupboard under the stairs were listed as 'brooms, various, and miscellaneous rubbish from the past'. Miscellaneous rubbish from the past has its attractions as a definition of history, but it also reads very like a sentence of execution on the original manuscript of Jacques le Balleur's *Monthly Reports*.

The details given by Jacques of his experiences before 1559 (the beginning of his life with the Tupinilis) can for the most part be confirmed from contemporary sources. The most important documents are *Les Singularitez de la France Antarctique* by André Thevet, a Franciscan friar who was one of the original party sailing from France in July 1555 under the command of Nicolas Durand de Villegagnon; and *Histoire d'un voyage fait en la terre du Brésil* by Jean de Léry, who like Jacques himself was one of the Calvinists recruited in Geneva during 1556.

The island in the bay of Rio de Janeiro, which was Jacques's home during 1557–8, had been chosen by

Villegagnon as the base from which he would attempt to establish a French presence in Brazil. He called it Fort Coligny in honour of the great Gaspard de Coligny, Admiral of France, who had supported the expedition and had given it a secondary purpose, that of providing a haven for persecuted French Calvinists, or Huguenots, whose religious persuasion Coligny shared. No trace remains of the primitive settlement and fortifications described by Jacques le Balleur. The island is now the headquarters of the National Naval Academy of Brazil.]

THE MONTHLY REPORTS

[Each entry represents a single tobacco leaf, da Caminha to his credit having made it plain in his edition where one leaf ended and the next began. The date in each case is that of the new moon at which the entry was written.]

[11 April 1559]

O Lord and Saviour Jesus Christ, Only Begotten and Beloved Son of Almighty God, I thank You from the depths of my heart that You have singled out Your humble servant Antoine de la Taille to bring the gospel news to the savages of this New World.

[The name de la Taille does not feature in other sixteenth-century accounts of the French in Brazil, but it transpires from the *Monthly Reports* that he was a Huguenot minister of extreme zeal who joined Jacques le Balleur and the other Calvinists on their way through Paris to the French coast. He set off alone into the Brazilian interior early in 1558.]

Chastise in me O Lord the sins of vanity and pride, but I am reminded today how once You did use for Your own purposes a certain Constantine, making him a humble brother in Christ and instrument of Your merciful will, even while he held sway as Roman emperor over countless kingdoms and principalities. Thus was much of the old world brought at that time within Your tabernacle.

And, after the old world, a new one? Do You now turn inside out Your former method, as one might a seamless robe, transforming not emperor into Christian but Christian into emperor? Today I am, as it were, crowned and anointed emperor of some five hundred souls – which souls, by my new authority and Your eternal grace, shall most emphatically be saved.

My consecration – forgive me, Lord – was like that of some priestly king in the days of Israel. Unguents, a towering mask with wide, all-seeing eyes which covered mine and made me blind, gentle hands guiding me through richly scented places to some inner sanctum, instructions to remove the mask when my attendants had left. And they told me that when I found myself alone I was to write, for that has always been part of their sacred rituals. Writing! A holy act in this savage place! They are Yours, Lord, they shall be Yours.

I heard the last of them leave the chamber. I lifted off the mask. Before me was a large green leaf, a stick of wood shaped at one end almost like a quill, and a dish of a thick black liquid. I had been told to cover with writing both sides of the leaf and then to put on the mask and step forth from this sanctuary. Thus have You ordained, Lord, that there may be preserved in writing, on this great occasion, the text of my prayer.

Bring them Your peace, O Lord. They may have the innocence of savages, but savages they are. Of that I have ample proof before me as I write. It was some minutes before my eyes grew accustomed to this dark inner room of woven reeds, but then I saw for the first time why almost no light filtered through the wall facing me. It is packed tight, like a poultry shop before Epiphany, with row upon row of tiny human heads – I know not how they are so small – pierced from ear to ear and squashed together on long wooden rods. These must be their enemies, captured in battle. No doubt the bodies of these unfortunates were roasted, on the spits which the savages call *boucans*, and then were eaten by the tribe with much carousing. For such is the custom of these people.

It *has* been the custom, Lord, but with Your divine Grace it shall be no more. You have placed these heads here, my subtle Saviour, casting them before me as a challenge to strengthen my resolve, and as a measure of the task in hand. I have reached the bottom of the second side of this leaf. I step forth now to fulfil Your demands.

[If da Caminha had grasped even the rudimentary task of editing, he would have informed the reader that this first *Monthly Report* was in a different hand, as indeed it must have been, from the second and all succeeding ones.]

[10 May 1559]

Lord, I am a sinner. You do not need me to tell You that Jacques le Balleur is a sinner. From sudden death, O Lord, preserve us. So have I often prayed, never thinking to ask why suddenness should not be a blessing, but I understand now. You have surprised me with the hour of my death, but You have mercifully given me time – and a leaf, and a quill of sorts – to settle my account.

The breaking of my monastic vows. I must not repent of this. They were made in blind error to the scarlet woman of Rome, the whore of Babylon herself. We know from countless signs that You look with favour upon the reformers of Your holy Church, and that You have, as it were, brought the ark of the covenant to rest in Geneva. But, Lord, we men are often confused. Three left the monastery together, of whom I was the youngest and the least learned. So, if there was any trace of error in our leaving, I beseech Your mercy in my hour of need. It was done with good intentions.

Fornication. This has been a weakness. You have planted strongly in me, Lord, the urge which old Adam first felt in his loins. Yet here too I may say I am of the reformed party. I sinned less in this respect after leaving the monastery. In Paris there was only the Sign of the Dappled Goose. In Geneva nothing. And in Fort Coligny less than nothing, for the five young girls brought over with us were marked for Villegagnon's men. Virtue therefore, except from time to time the sin of Onan. That, in the circumstances, You will surely understand. Have mercy on me, Lord.

I can truly say that I have not coveted my neighbour's house nor his manservant nor his ox nor his ass. His wife and his maidservant we have dealt with under fornication. Have mercy upon me.

I had believed they were bringing me here as if for a coronation, to be a leader among these savages (my only thought being that I might more fully work Your will).

24

There were ointments rubbed upon me by women with no anger in their eyes. There was a mask which looked fit for a king of savages. There were soft hands leading me, almost as if to bed. Only when I was alone in here did I see what fate they led me to.

You do not bring many of us, Lord, face to face with ourselves after death. We see in charnel houses and country graveyards the skulls of those who were once as we are. But a skull can never be our own face in a mirror. That is a change too great. From flesh to bone is from tragedy to philosophy. We may marvel or shudder at a skull, but it directs the mind to higher thoughts. And even if it leads us, when no one is watching, to press fingers into cheek, to seek out those hidden bones, to convince ourselves that they do indeed lurk, waiting in their turn to be revealed, yet we never really see ourselves in the skull or feel the skull in us.

But looking now at the head of the very reverend Antoine de la Taille, even though I last saw him almost two years ago, even though from topknot to chin he is by some sorcery become little more than the width of my hand, even though he is blotchy blue and crimson and at one and the same time shrunken and puffy, like the pig's bladder of a fool found in a corner after the festivities are done, even with all that, as I stare into the half-face that remains to him, I see my own, my own tomorrow. And I do not marvel or shudder. I groan. Seeing myself in him I vomit from stomach to throat a fearful groan, as You intended. And I repent.

He is spiked through his ears, last on a rod with many others, savages all of them, killed and reduced like him but longer ago, brown and dusty beside his new puce.

There is space on the rod beside him. He and I shall await Your judgement cheek by jowl, closer even than when we knelt side by side in the crowded cabin of the *Grande Roberge* giving our thanks to You after an Atlantic storm. Closer than that by far. We listened then to Maître Richier as he preached of Your mighty wrath.

It was for Your sake, Lord, that Antoine de la Taille came to Brazil, for Your sake that I very largely came, to bring to these people the news of Your infinite wrath and Your even more infinite (for You, yes for You, beyond infinity is surely possible) mercy. Sieur de la Taille and I, ear to ear, shall await Your summons. Merciful Lord, spare us Your wrath.

[9 June 1559]

Astonishment. Relief. (And gratitude, Lord.) At finding myself in this sanctuary for another new moon. Sieur de la Taille has changed in these four weeks. Less red and blue. More green.

There are certain details to confess, but I had no choice. 'No choice? What was the alternative, my child? Was it death?' So my old confessor would invariably ask at such an excuse. 'And what of the saints?'

I am not a saint, nor ever planned to be. No real choice. Judge for yourself. [Da Caminha seems to have followed quite faithfully Jacques's use of upper or lower case. An apparently unconscious but consistent pattern emerges according to whether he feels he is addressing

26

the Lord or some imagined human reader.] Yes, judge you may. I will set down on this leaf what happened, and nothing extenuate.

After one last prayer, with my account up to that time settled as well as might be, I looked round this sanctuary – more at the lattice work of light through the reeds than at the shrunken heads, for I was thinking that these images, if the savages should strike me down as I stepped out, would be my last glimpse of this friendly earth – and then I slowly brought the tall mask down over my head. Darkness. I paused. Then pushed open the door. And awaited the blow.

Someone took my right hand, gently. Someone took my left hand. There was silence. I could not tell whether two or more were in front of me. Then, still very gently, they seemed to be pulling me forward. Pulling me on to something? A poisonous snake, sacred executioner in their savage ritual? My feet were bare. I lifted them high with each step and lowered them as if the ground were paved with broken glass, hoping to become aware of the creature before arousing him. Or a deep pit? Now I slid each foot slowly over the ground, the toes seeking for a sheer edge or other lurking trap. Still the pressure was only gentle, almost tentative. But my captors could see what lay ahead of me and were no doubt enjoying the anticipation of my death.

Then they turned me, swinging me slowly like a boat on the tide, and my back nudged against what seemed to be a pillar. Now I perceived the detail of my fate. Someone undid my shirt and slipped it down over my arms. They joined my hands behind the pillar and tied them. Soft cords. Never violent or hasty. They were making the most of this ceremony. And still there was an uncanny silence.

Death at the stake. Nothing unusual. The ground seemed flat, no brushwood around my feet, so I was to be spared the flames. I praised the Lord for that. I have ever had a dread of the heretic's death, even at the hands of uncomprehending savages. But such an end was unlikely here, for it would reduce my head to no fit company for Sieur de la Taille. A garrotte was impossible while the mask remained in place. It must be a dagger, or arrows. I was praying to You, Lord (in Latin as well as French I freely confess), and the well-worn phrases were tumbling faster even than Brother Jerome's before Sunday breakfast.

But then they seemed to insist on an indignity such as we Christians would never impose on a condemned man. I felt nimble fingers at the cord about my waist. Others were unfastening my breeches. I paused in my prayers to roar a protest at these lewd savages. My words echoed mightily inside the mask and I expected a sudden blow in retaliation, a stroke of martyrdom for Your sake.

Instead, in the silence after my bellow, a most unexpected sound. That special almost rasping noise that comes in the throats of young women when several together are trying not to laugh out loud. What was this?

My breeches were around my knees. One foot was lifted, then the other, and they were off. Hands were fumbling at the knot I tie in the string of my undergarment. It seemed they could not pick it apart. They tugged this way and that. By this time there was open laughter, women's laughter. Then someone must have used a knife. Suddenly the waistband was slack. And I was naked.

Silence. Prolonged silence. Was this the moment? How many of these savages were staring at me? I was ready now to leave this world, naked as the day I entered it except for the absurd mask. But was I to be despatched by *women*?

Fingers touched the inside of my knee. Slowly they ran up my thigh and ended their exploration by circling with a flourish round my navel. Something wet was against my shoulder. It slithered down my arm, mysterious and unrecognisable until little teeth nipped me above the elbow. And then, most startling of all, a hand gently cupped me from below, as delicately as if judging the weight of a pair of new-laid eggs.

And suddenly I remembered. In the pages of Maître Rabelais, the pages I had with me when these savages found me, Friar John says to Panurge: *Would thou be content to be found with thy Genitories full in the Day of Judgement?* They were following the text, my own text, my own last will and testament as it must have seemed to them. Before the blow of the dagger, or the hail of arrows, they were employing their womenfolk to do me this last courtesy. In the moment of understanding their design I determined to resist.

But this is one part of Your creation, Lord, where conscious thought, even though it may of a sudden start the process, has ever proved incapable of preventing the completion of that same process. Those hands, and there seemed to be many, were at that moment the tyrants of my destiny. With the mere remembrance – or is it anticipation? – these genitories feel . . . But the leaf too is full, written in every corner.

[8 July 1559]

I begin to grow impatient with Maître Rabelais. I almost wish I had not bought his four little volumes as we passed through Troyes. They were in the bookshop of Monsieur Loys, newly printed that month, every word clear even though printed small. The very thing for a traveller on a long voyage, each open volume sitting easily in the hand and all four slipping together into a pocket.

[This is no idle boast by Jacques, from an age of more primitive technology. Surviving copies of this exquisite little edition put to shame our own printing standards. The paper is as if new yesterday, the type clear and black and tiny. The page size is only $4'' \times 2\frac{1}{2}''$ (10×6 cm) and the four volumes together will fit into a box less than $2''$ wide. Here is almost the whole of Rabelais – the short final volume of doubtful authenticity was published after the Calvinists sailed for Brazil – perfectly legible, indeed a delight to the eye, in a space that otherwise might be occupied by about half a pound of cheese. Jacques was right to be impressed.]

The little books had pride of place in the centre of Monsieur Loys's window. I thought of the volumes we had with us. Several copies of the Bible. Prayer books. The *Institutes* of Maître Calvin. *On the Lord's Supper* by

Zwingli, with his *Commentary on True and False Religion*. Others of this kind. Heavy books. Very different from jesting Rabelais, a man after my own heart for he too was a religious who felt the pangs of lechery. (Unlike me he felt also the need for authority. He travelled to Rome and returned with formal permission to keep a concubine. A papal bull for fornication, not transferable. In my old monastery we preferred to copulate and confess. What else had we to mention?)

We spent the night in Troyes, and the next morning the little books were mine. They remained hidden in my pocket until we were well out to sea, but after that everyone – except the three ministers, Richier, Chartier and de la Taille – was eager to borrow them.

So now I have to read every day, two or three times at least, the same ten pages – *Round-headed Cod, Figging Cod, Spruce Cod, Plucking Cod*, strange gospel indeed – to the young savage Topi Noi, to whom de la Taille taught French. *Bouncing Cod, Levelling Cod, Fly-flap Cod*, this was not my intention, Lord. Yet I am coming to believe that it *was* Your intention, part of Your mysterious design.

Did You direct my eyes to the window of Monsieur Loys? Was it at Your prompting that I spent almost my last *sous* on those four little books? And how could it be, unless at Your express command, that from the thousands of pages which crossed the ocean with us in the *Grande Roberge* only those ten should reach these people hungry for Your word?

The answer is clear. It is Your divine purpose to draw them towards You with words, holy or not so holy, to which they will respond. The *Institutes* of Maître Calvin would not, I fear, amuse young Topi Noi. You chose, in Your infinite wisdom, the ten pages that would be closest – uncommonly close I begin to see – to the interests and customs of the savages. It is the way we teach children. Once their attention is held, they can be introduced to higher truths. And for that higher purpose, I now understand, You have chosen me, fornicator past and present, to be Your instrument. Lord, give me strength.

In this last month – I speak of moons only, for I am lost already as to May or June – I have been alarmed by one particular passage in those pages of Rabelais. When I was blindfold and staked, that first time, and it seemed that Saracca and the other girls were intent only on sweeping the granary by hand before my execution, I thought of the single sentence, *Would thou be content to be found with thy Genitories full in the Day of Judgement?* But when, instead of a sudden death, there were sweet games, day and night, not suitable for describing here, my fears turned instead to other sayings elsewhere in the same pages:

> therefore do I promise, that from henceforth no Malefactor shall by Justice be executed within my Jurisdiction who shall not, for a day or two at least before, be permitted to culbut, and foraminate, Onocrotal-wise, that there remain not in all his vessels, to write a great Greek Y; such a precious thing should not be foolishly cast away; he will perhaps therewith beget a Male, and so depart the more contentedly out of this Life, that he shall have left behind him one for one. [See page 173, lines 55–63.]

Culbut and foraminate, these are Rabelaisian words for pleasant deeds commonly expressed with fewer letters, and though I know not how the *Onocrotal* [pelican] may do it, I am sure he can devise no improvement upon the methods of my concubines.

Saracca plays mistress of ceremonies. It is her seeming determination to ensure that nothing remains in all my vessels which brings to mind the passage quoted above. And then I fear again for myself. Am I the condemned Malefactor who shall not be executed unless *for a day or two at least before* I am permitted to *culbut and foraminate*? My enjoyment turns again to dread, so much so that at times I have risked disappointing those pleasant girls. *A day or two at least* is a loose phrase, a vilely loose phrase, Maître Rabelais, though *at least* may seem to imply an open-ended period. Sometimes I tremble still. In Your hands be it, O Lord.

[7 August 1559]

Here is a paradox. These people cannot write, and yet writing to them is sacred. A written leaf, such as I now make, is a holy object. Saracca will take this leaf (after the first foramination of the new moon, never before) and will place it in a secret house where none but she, the senior of my wives, may enter. In there, she tells me, are a thousand and more leaves, the work of so many months, each written in this same sanctuary by one of their kings before myself.

These texts are their most sacred treasures. By this You make plain to us, Lord, that these seeming savages are of a reformed disposition. They bring to holy writ, as we of Geneva do, the care and veneration which the corrupt minions of Rome lavish upon a lump of the clay left over after You had fashioned Adam, or a long red hair recalling the earthly charms of the Magdalen, or even, dread Lord, and I remember this with revulsion from my misguided youth, parings from Your own sacred fingernails and portions of Your blessed foreskin, all other recoverable elements having ascended with You as the Scriptures prove.

These savage people admittedly keep the relics of their kings – their wizened faces with Sieur de la Taille confront me now – but they do not venerate such remains. These, they rightly say, are but the earthly remnants of the royal house and will come at last to dust. But their spirits live, so they believe, through the power of the writing on the leaves.

But what, you may ask (you? who? I write for myself alone, and even I am not permitted to see these words again), what, it may be asked, can have been written on those thousands of leaves by savages who cannot write? It seems that the kings have inscribed there what they take to be the names, or signs, of those who have preceded them. A name of this kind is marked on the wooden rack beneath each of the shrivelled heads. At the new moon the king, writing in this sanctuary as I do now, would copy the marks below each head, working back from the most recent and fitting in as many as the leaf would allow. Any whose name was included would live in spirit through the coming month.

Saracca tells me that each king, just before his death, must write on a small leaf his own spirit's name, chosen no doubt from the many symbolic marks with which he has become familiar, and must give this leaf to the senior wife. She gives it to the next king, and he will copy the new name on to the wooden bar below the dead man's head. And thus has this not unreasonable custom of the savages continued.

It seems that Sieur de la Taille refused to write his name, intending no doubt by this act that the monarchy should remain French and reformed. The new reign could not begin, according to their notions, without his name being written, but no one unless of our party would know that name, first speaking it to satisfy the savages and then showing it in letters. And so came I, as part of Your design, to this pleasant and lascivious throne.

It is, I think, two months since I wrote DE LA TAILLE on the strip of wood. I would not have wished his family to have seen him then. He was at his worst, and in his condition I foresaw my own. But now he is much recovered, as sometimes an apple after a squashy middle period will shrink and dignify itself into a wrinkled antiquity.

Saracca will not tell me of what he died. But his illness must have been of an intimate nature. Whenever I ask, it causes my wives, who were also his, to blush and giggle and to say there there, never mind that.

[5 September 1559]

A pattern emerges. I am like a woman now, for my life follows the moon. I can lay out my month as regular and as predictable as a church calendar.

Day 1. Today. The first day after the moon, like a baited bull, has turned its horns in one swift flick from right to left. This, Lord, is Your sign to these savages that once again You will increase Luna to a fatness which they take to signify prosperity. The tall mask is placed upon my head and I am led in here. The leaf and the ink await me. I complete my text (writing whatever I wish, for they consider the magic of our writing superior to their old list of kings), and then I step forth as the centrepiece, almost the brazen idol, of their sweet rituals. Always the same beginning, blind at the stake, teasing fingers, soft palms. I must not dwell on that for fear of anticipation.

Day 1 to Day 14. After the first foramination, no matter with whom, Saracca cries out with a throbbing sound, more like a gurgle though as high almost as a scream, rising from the courtyard of my palace to echo round the open space outside, which I last saw full of the men of the tribe in solemn display as they prepared to lower the mask over my face.

All my wives now back away from me, and I must sit in a bright cotton throne which hangs from the branch of a tree (these people sleep in cotton bags, suspended in like manner). I am surely, as I sit there in all the solemnity I can muster, the only naked king enthroned in Christendom – for Christendom I count this place to be, for Your sake. Saracca now fetches my written leaf and takes it to the secret house where only she may enter.

I shall never see it again, and so cannot tell what I may in the past have written. Forgive me, Lord, if there have been indelicacies.

When Saracca returns, all formality ends. I am then, in our games, but as one among my subjects, albeit all the subjects here are female and to my eye, who have ever liked brown skins, uncommonly pretty. My wives have sleek black hair on their heads but none on their bodies, for there they pluck out every young hair as soon as it shows, much as we say that to pluck out young sins before they are fully formed is the painless path to virtue. They wished at first to work upon me the same improvement but I protested that mine were like long-established customs, grown too deep for painless removal. Moreover mine are reddish in hue which I was able to present as a rare curiosity, so I am still in possession of them and believe that I have become, even in this small respect, much cherished.

For these two weeks we play as we please. Or, to be more precise, I play and it is their desire to please. I will not elaborate except to say that things were never thus at the Dappled Goose. No other man is allowed into this palace of mine, which has been stocked with the choicest morsels of food and liquor that their native customs can provide.

They make their liquor in a manner singularly appropriate to a temple of Venus. My sweethearts chew the root from which it is made, disgorging the moistened pulp into a common vat where it will bubble and ferment. The result may not equal the crushed grapes of Bordeaux or the apples of Normandy, but it adds gaiety to our celebrations.

Day 15. By some magic, I know not what, my twenty darlings, at the full moon or very close to it, all together commence their sanguinary flux. It signifies the end of revelry, though to tell the truth in the previous few days I have often come to feel sated and they jaded. It is during these last days that I am able to bring them the good news, Lord, of Your brief life on earth and Your merciful atonement for the sin of Adam. Thus are we slowly becoming a Christian community, though a visitor newly arrived from Geneva might detect unorthodoxy.

Another paradox. My task in saving these savage souls to dwell for eternity with You involves, if strictly interpreted, endangering by concupiscence my own chances of that same everlasting bliss. But how should I repent, Lord, of this necessary act, or many acts, leading as they do to so good an end? I repent only that I cannot avoid finding pleasure in what stricter teachers have considered a sin.

Augustine puzzled at length, so I was taught, as to how You expected Adam in the Garden of Eden to fulfil Your main requirement of him (that he should begin the long process of *culbut and foramination* which would at length people the earth) while not being susceptible to those sweet pangs which for us precede the act but which became known to him only through disobedience, eating the forbidden fruit. Had You intended Adam to disobey? That was impossible. The learned Bishop of Hippo decided after long cogitation that You must have intended Adam and his descendants, living without sin, to possess the mechanical means for an enlargement of the member, as required for the act, without any of the accompanying sensations which Augustine himself so strongly felt and as strongly repented. I am no August-ine, and never planned to be. I set to with a will, Lord, in whatever task You place before me. For my justification I have faith in You alone.

[Jacques is recalling, in a much abbreviated but not inaccurate form, the arguments of *The City of God*, Book XIV, chapter xxiv, 'That our first parents, had they lived without sin, should have had their generative members as much subject to their wills as any other limb', and chapter xxvi, 'That our first parents in Paradise might have produced mankind without any shameful appe-tite.']

At the full moon my wives remain in the palace (I call it palace, though even our player kings at home would hardly deem it such), but I am myself at this same time returned, wearing my mask, to the outer world of male responsibilities. A dish is placed in my hands and Saracca guides me through a doorway of hanging fronds. Outside is a platform giving on to the public square. When I appear a shout of approval goes up from the assembled villagers (none but men). My mask is lifted off, and on the first occasion I was mightily perplexed to find myself carrying a bowl of fruit. But it has a meaning, and one not unflattering to myself. The fruit changes according to the season. Last month's resembled figs.

Topi Noi is beside me on the platform, and now he throws the pieces of fruit one by one into the crowd, counting in their own language. The men cram it into their mouths, laughing as they do so, while the juice runs down their chins.

Each month the number of pieces of fruit varies. I shall not explain exactly how this number is arrived at, nor who counts. Suffice it to say that it depends on my prowess, and that preparing myself now to step through the door and to celebrate the new moon with my wives, I feel that this coming month there will be more fruit in the dish than ever before.

Fortunately, though this was a very large leaf, I am now at the end of it. For I sense in myself a great impatience.

[5 October 1559]

I have been reminding myself all month of where I left off and where I must begin.

Day 15 to Day 29. After the distribution of the fruit – nineteen pieces this last month, of a large red kind which they call *pasimenan* [persimmon] – I go with Topi Noi and the others to the French house. 'French house' sounds odd in the jungle, but that is their name for it and it is the best description.

Topi Noi has chosen nine boys of his own age or younger (he tells me he is seventeen) and he is determined that they shall all learn French from me just as he himself did from Sieur de la Taille, who when they were together would allow no word between them of any other language. We have the same rule in the house – at present a small and almost derelict shelter to one side of the village clearing, but Topi Noi is planning something better. Any boy who utters there a word of Tupinili is rewarded by Topi Noi with a slap on the cheek, often quite hard. This is their manner of correction among themselves, and they accept it willingly.

Topi Noi. A strange boy, or man. Since the day that he and the others discovered me on the river bank, he has been my guide and my gaoler but never quite my friend. Without him I would not be alive, would not be king, would not be able thus to do Your holy work among these people. I have never once, in all the months of my stay here, set foot in any direction not planned for me by this same Topi Noi. If he so decided, as we both know, these people would roast and eat me just as they will one day roast and eat their prisoner Ramram Ghi, who now copulates tethered among them (as I do).

It is difficult to like Topi Noi. Or his disgusting habits. All the men here wear bones (from the spines of animals) in holes in their lower lips. These look like leaky plugs, or oozing corks, for the spittle dribbles out around them. But the other men at least keep their bungs in place. It is Topi Noi's peculiar fancy to remove his, when thinking deeply or preparing an argument, and to stick his tongue through the aperture, running it round the edges with a look of greedy enjoyment, as if his dank orifice were the rim of a honey pot. For all his brilliance, he lacks charm.

The morning passes in lessons at the French house. Each day I start by reading the ten pages of the Book. *Thumping Cod, Bumping Cod, Tumbling Cod, Berumpling Cod* . . . They join in every 'Cod' with a liturgical vigour which would put to shame the mumblings of my monastery friends. And a few begin now to memorise

41

the epithets and repeat them with me. *Vigorous Cod, Clashing Cod, Wagging Cod.* After this litany we come to the text itself, beginning:

> *My Harcabuzing Cod, and Buttockstirring Ballock, Fryar John, my Friend: I do carry a singular respect unto thee, and honour thee with all my Heart, thy Counsel I hold for a choice and delicate Morsel* [lines 13–16]

I address this to Topi Noi, who sits at my right hand. As a result he has become known to all now as Friar John.

Then we go through the text and I elucidate as best I may (just as our teachers did with Your Book, Lord), for like You this Rabelais has passages not clear at once to the untutored mind. Indeed he uses many words unknown to me, so that often, to keep the trust of these my followers, I must improvise.

After the daily reading – and several can already repeat whole passages with me, though ignorant of what the separate words may mean – we come to the morning instruction in our French tongue. Thus am I professor here of both Theology and Language. The boys point at different articles – their nose, an arrow, the roof – screaming at me to tell them, them first, 'Me me me', the name in French. I am assailed with a chorus of 'What is, what is, what is?' and a small forest of waving arms.

To preserve discipline in my classroom I have made them sit in a row facing me on a bench (a fallen tree dragged here for the purpose), as French boys would. They make, I must tell you, a strange sight. They are naked, as savages will be, except in one important respect. It is the custom here to tie a piece of cotton round the foreskin, as if to keep safe at home the *Round-headed Cod*. With this string in place they would consider themselves dressed for High Mass in Notre-Dame, yet without it they feel shame to be so much as glimpsed by their mother-in-law. Such is the tyranny of fashion.

So in front of me they sit, my eager scholars, and between their thighs there hang, with pinched and beribboned ends, what most resemble nine small black puddings of Bresse. Black-pudding Cod. Here is a theme unthought of even by Maître Rabelais.

[3 November 1559]

I do not believe these savages will eat me. Or do me any other harm. *A day or two at least* has spun out to many months.

I have, then, my stay of execution. And in its place? The sentence is commuted to perpetual imprisonment. Even if I could find my way back down the great cliffs from this hidden valley, what would await me near the coast? The Chevalier de Villegagnon? He drowned three of our party for heresy and would make short work of me. Or the Portuguese, having perhaps driven off Villegagnon and the French? Death at Portuguese hands would hardly be preferable.

So this place would seem to be my prison for life. Yet what does that mean? It is surely a prison that many would choose. Prolonged fornication, at certain seasons, for a moral and holy purpose. My every wish tended to in one place by willing handmaidens, while elsewhere I enjoy the challenges of the intellect in male company, with ten faithful disciples to assist me in the unravelling of scriptural niceties. Tolerable and plentiful food. No great need of clothes. And for my diversion the pleasures of the chase, for while the moon declines from full to new we spend our afternoons, when lessons are over, hunting with the men of the tribe.

Prison?

Only in the sense that I may not be elsewhere. Yet there were people in my village of Thierry-le-Bois who lived a contented lifetime without travelling as far as the castle of Labrède, less than three leagues distant [approx. 9 miles, 14 km]. There often passed through this village, on the way to Santiago de Compostela, pilgrims whose horizons were without limit. I remember one who had handled the bones of the Magi in Cologne, had kissed old Peter's toe in Rome, had marvelled at Your empty tomb, Lord, in Jerusalem, and now was wearing the cockle-shell for the second time as he trudged on a return visit to James, brother of John, in Compostela.

Even confronted by such travellers, our villagers never considered setting foot beyond Thierry-le-Bois (except to Valmonay on Tuesdays). And the reason why they did not want to leave? Because they were free to do so. These were freemen, not bound to any master or any piece of land, and they exercised their freedom in staying put.

The lord of Valmonay himself did not enjoy idle luxury such as mine here, and a pilgrim must travel to the land of the Turk to find another palace where fornication is a policy of state, as it is in mine. I would be a poor philosopher to fret at these prison walls.

There is one way in which I do feel constrained. I am a prisoner of silence. There is no word of me. To the outside world I must seem to have vanished. It may be that Christians will one day find me alive here, and whether French Papists or Portuguese they would perhaps preserve me for the tale I can tell. I might travel then from court to court, entertaining real kings with news of this savage kingdom of mine. I might instruct young ministers in the method of spreading Your word among primitive peoples. I could publish pamphlets, and heads would turn when I arrived for divine service.

But if I die here, undiscovered, all that I have done will be as nothing. There will be no report of Jacques le Balleur. A reformed Frenchman who disappeared into the jungle of Brazil. Presumed dead. Gone to his Maker.

In this prison of silence there is one small chink. These leaves. They are safely kept, a thousand months and more Saracca says, perhaps several centuries of them already. Here will my story lie, like a forgotten bag of seed in a dark corner of a granary, awaiting discovery and a new existence in the outside world.

I imagine a reader, *you*, a hundred years from now, let us say in the year of our Lord 1650, reading in your home in Paris these words, transcribed by a scholar from the dried leaves and printed as firm and clear as the scurrilities of Maître Rabelais. You live surrounded, I have no doubt, by modern conveniences. No more need, perhaps, to carry oil for the lamp up several flights of stairs. Instead, a pipe has been laid under the streets by the reformed city fathers (no more Sorbonne, pot-pourri of persecuting Papists). In this reformed pipe, oil flows. From every tenement a long wick descends in a tube, sucking up the oil to feed the lamps. I do not know how you pay for this oil.

Let us not worry about payment. Turn up the wick, settle down comfortably in your chair, and read now the amazing story and wonderful adventures of Jacques le Balleur.

If you are there.

[3 December 1559]

Jacques le Balleur. Born about 1515 in the Gironde, son of a priest and a laundrywoman. Sent as a small child to the monastery in Thierry-le-Bois. A voice as high and as clear as a mountain stream, so the monks would tell me – I croak now like an amorous frog, You give, Lord, and You take away – so I was always a favourite with brother choirmaster.

I remember I joined the choir the year that Maître Luther married his nun. [He married Catherine von Bora in 1525.] The fuss that caused! Buzz buzz every day on the refectory benches from the moment the reading was finished. He had done it 'to spite the devil', so the fat monks said, and laughed. I could not understand why they laughed so much. Were we not to spite the devil? He certainly seemed to have his way without spite or respite in this monastery of ours, where at any moment you might meet a vegetable woman or a seamstress or a

46

broom lady or a dairymaid hurrying along a corridor or up a flight of stairs, far from her place of business and no apparent reason why. We heard later that Martin and Catherine, Marty and Kate, Momo and Kiki (how the old monks did laugh) had produced a large family. And I thought lucky children, with a home that was not a monastery.

From choirboy to novice, from novice to monk. The easiest path, like a mountain stream flowing downhill. But flowing towards old Shitterpot (Father Joseph or Reverend Father, the new abbot at the time, to address him more respectfully), who never saw things my way, particularly after the affair of the placards. I must have been eighteen then. [Or nineteen; it was in 1534 that these 'placards' were posted up in many French towns, attacking the Roman form of the Mass.] I saw some of them in the house of a man in Valmonay – later they burnt him – and every complaint printed there against the overpotent po-pissed pope in Rome was also a complaint of mine against this Shitterpot on our own doorstep in Thierry-le-Bois.

Even so, it was some years before I left. I wasted the lustiest part of my youth with introit, terce and nones (though I admit I had my share of *culbut and foramination* up narrow stairs and down dark monastery passages), until one evening there was a large meeting organised in the woods by that same martyr of Valmonay.

I persuaded four friends, older and quieter in the monastery's ways than myself but game still for a sally forth, and we slipped out. They had at the meeting a preacher, fiery with promises to all who would join his party and with talk of secret houses of refuge in Lyons and Paris and other cities. On our return to the monastery, we found we had been discovered. Two stayed to face Shitterpot's rage, but I and two others slipped out again into the night. Reformed.

If I have ever been worthy of You, Lord, it was during those years. Zeal and danger served then only to increase each other. My new friends were devout in a manner previously unknown to me. I liked them, and began a little to grow like them. We felt we were in the tradition of Baptist John, preparing for Your kingdom on earth.

Yet I found myself surrounded still by the wickedness of the world. In my weakness I confess that I found this a comfort, a comfort which would be singularly lacking in Geneva – no sign of a dappled goose there. But the persecuting king [Henry II] and the evil professors of the Sorbonne were stoking the fires for us, and prudence dictated that we find a safer address. I left for Geneva with a party of about twenty-five. Of these, two sailed later with me to Brazil.

And in Geneva? More bonfires. We cannot have been there a year before Michael Servetus arrived from Lyons. He had escaped from a papist prison – they had to be content in Lyons with burning him in effigy – and he sought refuge now, as we all did, in Geneva. Whereupon Maître Calvin slaps on him his own charge of heresy and new faggots are gathered.

We all talked endlessly (but very, very quietly) that autumn in Geneva [1553], arguing as to where this man's heresy lay. He had, we were told, novel ideas about the Trinity. But it seems to me, never a theologian, that this is entirely Your business, Lord. How You arrange things among Yourself is no concern of ours and must surely be all for the best. Servetus also said that when You walked on the earth, You had not mortal flesh, as we have, but some special celestial flesh, Yours and Yours alone. This was more disturbing – since all men devoutly wish, for comfort's sake, that You shall have been as like unto our own weak selves as is humanly, or divinely, possible. But either way, it was surely no burning matter.

Yet one bright autumn day [27 October] they set him alight, about a two hours' walk from the centre of Geneva. Thousands went, but I stayed in my lodgings and wished I were in some other place. Which is why I welcomed the man who came inviting Protestants to Antarctic France.

1560

I came as a carpenter. Your trade, Lord. It was tradesmen they required, with two ministers already enlisted.
Joinery had been my occupation in the monastery and
my livelihood thereafter.

There were some twenty of us, of whom I knew at
that time only two. André Lafon, a tailor. And Oyster
John, as we later called him, who was to act as clerk or
secretary, and who would spend much time with me in a
Tupinamba village near the coast. [This was Jean de
Léry: they discovered in the village that Léry was close to
the Tupinamba word for oyster, and the name stuck.]

We left Geneva in the autumn, three or four years ago
now [September 1556]. One spare horse for the baggage,
and that was mainly books. We went by Champagnole
to Dijon, then up through Chaumont to Troyes – the
Mount Sinai of the new religion here, for that was where
I found our Rabelaisian tablets.

Before Paris we visited Admiral Coligny at Châtillon.
Although a great man, indeed one of the mightiest in
France, he received us, tradesmen and pastors alike, with
reverence and courtesy, for he is known to look kindly
on our reformed faith although not openly of our party
[he declared himself a Huguenot two years later, in
1558]. The admiral told us that it was he who had urged
the Chevalier de Villegagnon to establish in Brazil a new
France, where men of our persuasion might live in peace.
To this end he praised our resolution, wished us God

speed and safe landing, and bid us share with him as a token of fellowship some good mulled wine of Burgundy. We left the next morning in high good spirits – except for Nicolas Carmeau, our cordwainer, who had helped the steward's boy in the disposal of the dregs.

We were in Paris nearly a month. (For old times' sake I sought out my dappled geese, but found all but two moved on and the place much changed.) Our purpose there was to gather up more pilgrims who would make with us this perilous journey, and it was in Paris that Sieur de la Taille joined us, our third minister. There were others, fine gentlemen, unreformed in faith and fallen upon hard times, whose interest seemed to be more in adventure and gain than in spreading Your gospel to the savages. There were six orphan boys, aged only about ten, who would be set to learning the American language, for at this age the brain is still soft and may easily take a new moulding. And there were five girls, at a guess not one of them more than sixteen years old, who were to marry in Brazil and people the New World with Frenchmen. Five young Eves for five old Adams among Villegagnon's men. There was to be no chance of a first bite of the apple during our voyage for they were accompanied by the formidable Madame Geneviève de Frontenac la Tour, a guardian powerful in resolve and by temperament excessively suspicious. Her basket of eggs would surely arrive uncracked; and so they did.

From Paris to Honfleur, where we embarked on three vessels. In one, the *Petite Roberge*, were the soldiers provided for our protection by the king (at the urging of Admiral Coligny). We were in another, the *Grande*

Roberge. And in the third, the *Rosée*, there travelled Madame Geneviève and her precious cargo. For two weeks all the passengers, papists and reformed, sinners and virgins alike, were at death's door with the illness which afflicts all who risk being tossed upon the ocean. It seemed that the very air we breathed was vomit.

Just as we were recovering, many of us were sickened anew by a different cause. We came up with two Portuguese vessels, possessed of fewer cannon than ourselves. Seeing our strength, they allowed us to board without a fight – whereupon the captain of the *Petite Roberge* ordered that all the food, all the sweet water, all the cargo (the sails even) from the smaller of their ships should be transferred to the larger, which would accompany us to Brazil. Meanwhile the Portuguese were placed in the empty vessel, to drift without sail or sustenance.

We protested, and the three ministers most vigorously among us, that this was certain death unless another Portuguese ship chanced upon them (small likelihood in this mighty ocean), which the captain agreed but said this was the custom at sea, where commodities are scarce and slow death on any voyage a strong possibility. Thanks to this transfer of goods, he said, we ourselves would be more likely to praise the Lord in a new land, albeit these Portuguese might now less probably do so. He added that the Portuguese and the French were never friends, and that they, had they the power, would have done the same to us. More charitable than this captain, calloused as he was by life at sea, we prayed together each morning in the *Grande Roberge* for the souls of those luckless Portuguese, that they might at their last breath come to see the error of their papistical ways.

It is true that we did nearly starve, for the rain got into our biscuit, breeding worms, and before journey's end many of us were as glad of a good fat meal-fed worm as at home we might be to see a snail or a frog set before us. There were storms, where we looked up in terror at a wall of sea. And we were nearly sunk by a mighty whale, a Leviathan of the kind You mentioned first to Job, which attacked us with a great jet of water and then tried to suck us down in a whirlpool to its own abode in the depth of the ocean, strewn with the carcasses of men of all nations and creeds.

Finally, after about four months, we set foot on shore [7 March 1557]. And – as seafarers often tell, but it remains hard to believe – the dry land itself was heaving like the sea.

[31 January 1560]

It is a strange custom that when a friendly vessel arrives near a port both those on the ship and those on land fire cannons at each other in greeting, as if to say we have the power to blow you to your Maker but for friendship's sake will aim short of the mark. Perhaps, while the bad aim is taken as a sign of present friendship, the cannon-balls themselves serve to warn that friendship is fragile. So it was with us at Fort Coligny. Peace proved as short as the gunners' aim.

The fort was on a small island in Guanabara Bay [now the seafront of Rio de Janeiro]. As a choice of home it had little to recommend it – not even a spring of fresh water, for which we settlers had to rely on the rain, collected in a large rock pool, full of weeds and lizards – but Villegagnon had selected it more for security than for comfort. It is barely a musket's shot from the coast, making simple our own expeditions inland but rendering us safe from sudden attack, for the many skills of the savages do not include seafaring.

After the salvoes we were rowed ashore from our three ships. The entire settlement had turned out to greet us on a rocky promontory near the water's edge. Most of the French looked like peasants, in clothing made ragged by toil, but there was a platoon of infantry in full uniform, perfect except for large patches of mildew; it was worn now for the first time since their own landing the previous year. More interesting, to our eyes, were the naked savages, many of them with painted chests, arms and faces, who had been pressed to help in the construction of the fort. While we looked at them with educated curiosity, they stared back at us wide-eyed and open-mouthed, as if we were so many men from the moon.

Then we noticed that their attention was not held by us men. They had eyes only for the five women. (You smile, you smirk even. But you are wrong. You are thinking in Parisian style.) We were told later of their astonishment at seeing women clothed. They had adjusted, over the years, to the sight of French or Portuguese men in tunic, doublet and hose. But these were the first of our women they had set eyes upon, and they had not until now considered that this strange burden of clothing might be imposed upon the female as well as the male form. They marvelled, and shook their painted half-shaven heads at human folly. (Seeing in my mind's eye Saracca and the others beyond that door, something in me marvels too at our elaborate fashions in clothing – though my lascivious girls might not fare so well on the shores of Lake Geneva in the month after Christmas.)

Raised above this strange crowd of full-dress soldiers and undressed savages, on a wooden platform supported by trestles, was the only figure in the group who would not have looked out of place in Geneva. He wore sober black, no frills, and a tall, tapering, broad-brimmed hat of the kind favoured by our ministers and by other leading citizens of proven virtue. This was the Chevalier de Villegagnon. By his appearance he seemed to make evident that his welcome was one of spiritual as well as practical comradeship. Behind him stood a young page, also in black, bearing a plump black cushion.

Villegagnon invited our ministers on to the platform beside him and begged them to conduct a seashore service of thanksgiving for our safe delivery. With due ceremony the page laid the cushion on the platform and Villegagnon knelt. After many heartfelt prayers each of the three ministers preached a short sermon of about half an hour. Thus were Your praises sung in the New World for the first time, Lord, according to the correct re-formed rite. At last, spiritually refreshed, we carried our belongings to the centre of the island.

So our arrival in Antarctic France seemed to promise well, with a noble leader visibly attached to true religion.

But we soon came to believe that it was the famed industry of Geneva, rather than its reputation for piety and doctrinal rectitude, which attracted the Chevalier and made him pose as one of us. For hardly had we arranged our baggage in the home allotted to us – a new-made shanty with a roof of reeds, looking about as waterproof as a Poitiers basket – when the order came that we should gather at the highest point of the island to carry stones for the construction of the fort and battery. Little did we think, as we piled stone upon stone, that some of us were constructing our own prison.

[29 February 1560]

This month there have arrived the first babies born (or known born), in the forty or more years of his life, to Jacques le Balleur. Two sons and a daughter. I can hardly believe their tiny perfection. I marvel each day at their fingers, their ears, their dimpled knees. Lord, that You should sculpt so small.

Telling you how I came here, and filling my leaves with Coligny this and Coligny that, my new life has crept on undescribed. I have asked repeatedly for a second leaf, but Saracca tells me their religion is strict on this point. One leaf each month, no more and no less, if the spirits of the dead are to rest content and the seasons to follow their course. And anyway, in view of what follows this monthly task, I might not have the patience for another leaf.

Nine months and more it must be since I sat here thinking I was about to die. Three of my wives have now given birth. Two others are nearly there, to judge by their beautiful bellies as they stand in my courtyard so relaxed, stomachs forward and shoulders back. And three more of the girls show signs. I feel like the patriarch Noah, landed here on my own Mount Ararat and peopling the world anew – as is Your intention, Lord, for these must be Christian children, and reformed. As they grow I shall teach them of Your strict mercy. At my knee they will learn French, while I, with these infants at their mothers' knees, will improve my understanding of their own Tupinili language.

Turn up the wick, burn more of the city fathers' oil (my dear reader, so far ahead in 1650), that I may ask you what improvements have been made in the matter of children's napkins? I remember a great stink and fuss in the Gironde, with cauldrons to seethe the offending tissues, vats of steaming ordure. Hurry now, and perhaps you may make a few *sous*, when I tell you that these savages in Brazil have discovered the answer which has for so long eluded our sophisticated French house-wives. Napkins disposed of after a single use, that is the secret. There grows in the jungle a large and very soft leaf which they wrap around the infant. In this all offensive matter is collected. When the leaf is removed from the child it is thrown (the leaf I mean) straight on to the fire which burns always in the courtyard of every house. What could be more simple? The men use the fire also, in place of a common privy, the embers being hot enough and thick enough to absorb immediately any amount of liquid with a hissing and a roaring which is the invariable accompaniment here to evenings of good fellowship. It is a cheering sight to see a circle of these topers, after untying their little ribbons, standing around the fire which sends red patterns dancing over their naked shapes, while together they deliver one element into the safe keeping of another.

Elements! There is much to tell you, and I would not have you believe that all is perfect with these people, for they are indeed abysmally ignorant. They believe there are five elements instead of four. To the four from which You, Lord, made all inanimate objects, namely earth, air, fire and water, these people have in their foolishness added metal, venerating it perhaps because they have so little of it. When I explain to them that metal is made of earth (for it is heavy) and of fire (for it will glow hot) and of water (for it can be brought to flow), indeed of all the four elements except air (for it will ever fall), they stare at me with open mouths like young birds in a nest.

Such is man's primeval innocence in matters of natural science, lacking the benefit of informed instruction. The task of a teacher is wearisome indeed, but most necessary.

[30 March 1560]

An astonishing thing has happened. Five minutes ago. Too soon to describe here. I shall write instead the passage which I have been planning all month, on the theme of holy writ and its interpretation. But I tremble

as I write. Tremble in case there has been a mistake.
Lord, You know my choice.

Performing Your wonders, O Lord, You move in a
mysterious way. (This was the sentence which I had
devised as my opening. Brief. Challenging. To the
point. With a hint of quotation. As we have been taught.
But it loses strength, I fear, coming now in second
place.) Mysterious indeed, for the virtues of Geneva, the
qualities of hard work and obedience which characterise
the citizens of that place, have come to this jungle valley
by means of a scriptural passage which is obscure in
interpretation but which has admirably served the
purpose.

In previous times the men of this tribe would mostly
sit about gossiping while pretending to work, such work
being perhaps the slow sharpening of the point of an
arrow or the mixing of poison in which to dip it. Now,
by the power of the text of Maître Rabelais and the
ever-growing authority of Friar John (the name Topi
Noi is all but forgotten) these same people labour every
daylight hour, digging foundations and dressing timber
for the parliament – as our new French house is to be
known.

The text, on which Friar John and the nine disciples,
together with myself, have spent many patient hours of
analysis, goes as follows:

> *therefore, my Billy, entertain as well as possibly thou canst,
> that Hypogastrian, lower sort of Troglodytick People, that
> their chief pleasure may be placed in the case of sempiternal
> labouring. Give order that henceforth they live not like idle
> Gentlemen, idle upon their Rents and Revenues, but that*

*they may work for their Livelyhood, by breaking ground
within the Paphian Trenches.* [lines 84–90]

From the very earliest days, long before the disciples
here knew the Book by heart, I was compelled during
my daily reading to explain any difficult word or phrase.
My misfortune has been that Maître Rabelais is very
much more learned than I. I do not know why the witty
Panurge (myself to these savages) is here addressed as
Billy, but Billy is now one of my titles. *Hypogastrian* is a
word of which I cannot remember the meaning, but
gastrian suggests stomach and so my early gloss – and
such details are never forgotten here – was that *Hypogastrian People* are those who are ever eager to fill their
stomachs. [Blunt's *Glossographia*, 1656: 'Hypogastrian
. . . belonging to that part of the belly which reacheth
from the Navel to the privy members.']

Troglodytick I was able to expound with confidence,
meaning as it does any small apartment, for it was used
once by a rich, sneering papist to describe my lodging in
Paris. As to *Paphian*, this is an epithet which I can claim
with certainty never to have stumbled upon, and I have
admitted as much from my very first reading of the text.
But Friar John has proved to the satisfaction of all that it
must relate to a word in their own language, *paipai* or
talking together, and that it is therefore linked to our
word 'parliament'. [*O.E.D.*: '1. Of or belonging to
Paphos, a city of Cyprus sacred to Aphrodite or Venus.
2. A devotee of the Paphian Venus; a prostitute.']

Thus is the text expounded now by Friar John. The
Hypogastrian, lower sort of Troglodytick People are the
ordinary men of the tribe who live in the cramped

quarters which are common in these villages, whose main thought is their next meal, and who have no word of French. Until now they have lived *like idle Gentlemen*, their *Rents and Revenues* being the natural produce which grows so freely here, any necessary work in that line being carried out by the women. *Henceforth* such gentlemen must *work for their Livelyhood*, accustoming themselves to *sempiternal* labour. *Sempiternal* I at hazard construed as doubly for ever, combining the Latin for 'always' with eternity. [In this case Jacques was right.] The project on which these gentlemen must work so hard and so long, Geneva-fashion, is precisely as stated in the text – *breaking ground within the Paphian Trenches*, which is digging the foundations for the new parliament.

I am not entirely happy, Lord, with this exposition, knowing as we do, You and I, that in the wider context Maître Rabelais was not here discussing village economy or the foundation of parliaments. But sometimes a wide context can be misleading. And even if the interpretation may seem by the highest standards insecure, its tendency is towards the good; and such a tendency we have been taught to consider, in moral philosophy, a mitigating factor.

So I have given them my blessing, Lord, and of course Yours. All the signs are that the building will be truly magnificent.

[28 April 1560]

I am in love. She is in her fifteenth year. She came with nothing but a thread round her waist, another at her wrist, and fifteen nuts in a cotton bag. I will tell you how.

These savage people each become one year older on the same day, for such is their custom, and that day is the first on which the nuts fall from a particular tree. They are like our horse chestnuts, but smaller, and it was my duty as king to distribute them, one to each.

I sat in the open space outside my palace with Friar John beside me, and between us a basket of conkers. Each member of the tribe passed before me, carrying cotton bags which I had not seen before. Friar John told me that these bags are their most precious possessions, containing all the nuts received in previous years. The people hide the bag in some secure place except for this one day, for to lose the bag is to lose all the years of one's life and so life itself.

When each had received a chestnut – I gave graciously, as a monarch should – he or she sat with friends laying out their store. There was much comparison and competition, measuring pile against pile as at the end of a game of draughts, for they respect age and to have the greatest number is counted an achievement.

Friar John boasted to me of an ancestor of theirs who once had a hundred and twenty conkers in his cotton bag. I told him this was nothing, for an ancestor of mine (who was also an ancestor of theirs) had lived about eight times as long as that. I could not remember the exact age, not having Your Book with me, Lord, but I improvised with authority and declared that the patriarch was buried with no less than nine hundred and ninety in his bag [Genesis 5: 27 – nine hundred and sixty nine]. I told them his bag was enlarged every hundred years to make room for the new collection, adding this detail to make the facts accord more fittingly with their own peculiar notions.

This was the first they had heard of Methuselah. Friar John immediately made a speech announcing the discovery of this impressive ancestor and praising the new Christian religion in general – Your name, Lord, is securely attached to our improvements here – and myself in particular for having brought him to their notice. Methuselah, Methuselah, this was the catch word everywhere that night.

At the end of the ceremony I gave Friar John his conker (I noticed that this brought his total to eighteen), and then he rose and made a formal speech to me – he requires no prompting, being a natural five-speeches-a-day man.

'*My dear friend Panurge, my Billy,*' he began in his usual convention, 'we know that in your country the years are not counted in chestnuts and so you came to us with *a wallet of lesser value than a beggar's scrip,* or no wallet at all.' He meant that I have no cotton bag of conkers to prove my age but he was quoting Rabelais – as he does on every possible occasion, often, as here, to no very good purpose. 'But now', he continued, 'you are our king and our *Superlative Cod,* and your years shall be numbered henceforth in chestnuts, O Methuselah among men.'

Methuselah he called me already, and soon I saw why. For he gave me now a cotton bag with conkers of my own and indicated that I should add one for this completed year. It seemed to me the largest bag in the village, and when I later counted I found that it contained no less than fifty-nine chestnuts.

Fifty-nine! Is this what they think of me? With seventeen pieces of fruit distributed among them this month, as also last month? What do they expect? *Do not here produce ancient Examples of the Priapaean Prowess of the fabulous Fornicators, Hercules, Caesar, and Mahomet, who in his Alchoran doth vaunt, that in his Cods he had the vigour of Threescore Bully Ruffians: but let no zealous Christian trust the Rogue, the filthy ribald Rascal is a Lyar.* [lines 142–9]

Fifty-nine years would be their guess for such a *Cod Superlative*? But no doubt it is not so much a criticism as a courtesy, to count the king the oldest and wisest among them.

After the ceremony of the conkers everyone sat in a circle and there was much rattling of instruments which they call *maraca*, being large dry hollow plants filled with seeds. These they shake in different rhythms to make a sound as sweet to their ears as the lute or psaltery to ours. Into the circle, moving to the sound of the maracas in patterns of sweet lascivious provocation, with shy but knowing smiles, naked except for a cotton thread round the waist and the wrist of each (according to their notions a sign of virginity), and each clutching fast her bag of chestnuts, came eleven of the beautiful girls of this tribe. Beautiful all of them, for such they are, particularly at this age (these eleven were those who had that day received their fifteenth chestnut).

But beautiful beyond all others one in particular. *Their*

eyes cast fetching glances here and there among the admiring crowd. Hers never broke from mine. However she doubled and spun, stamped her feet, unfurled her arms or curved her back, her head turned always so that it was towards me and I cannot remember even a blink to interrupt our gaze. She awaits me and I will fill this overlarge leaf with overlarge letters.

BEAUTIFUL ABOVE ALL OTHERS
TAIJÉ

[28 May 1560]

During the dance of the virgins Friar John explained that it was my duty as king to choose one of the girls for my palace. Choose? Taijé of the sparkling eyes, Taijé who can speak volumes with one turn of the head, Taijé with the arrow-shaped mole inside her left thigh which makes her laugh so much. Choice did not enter into it.

I planned in my mind the Tupinili words in which I would address her, for I have now learnt much of their language from my wives. 'I do not know your name' – Taijé, Taijé, there was a time, incredible as it seems, when my tongue never caressed my teeth and palate with those two successive sounds – 'but I know your beauty. Give me your hand.'

I never spoke those words. Friar John told me only to indicate my loved one, while they danced, and then there began – the dance continuing – the monthly ceremony of putting on my mask. As the unwieldy contraption was held above my head, ready to obliterate the swirling girls, I realised suddenly that there was to be no further process of selection. I whispered urgently to Friar John, 'Did you see the one?' 'Yes.' 'Are you sure?' But already the mask was down and I was blind, sensing the dance now only through the rhythm of the maracas. And then I was being led, as usual, through the palace to this sanctuary to write what I call my monthly report. As I wrote I had only one thought in mind. Will it be she? Did Friar John understand? Were there perhaps two girls in line when I pointed? Outside that door, would some other humdrum virgin await me?

I remember still the last words of my report that month: 'The signs are that the building will be magnificent.' I cared, and care, not a fig for the building. But my heart pounded with anticipation (and fear) as they led me to the stake. When I was aroused, and the mask removed, and while I still blinked in the sunlight, my eyes searched her out among my wives and she was not there. 'Where is she? Where is she?' Saracca laughed at my eagerness. With a caress she said: 'Soon. Soon you will go to her. For the moment you have only us, your old and faithful wives. We too deserve your love.'

Later I learnt this is another of their customs (they are a people much given to custom, Lord, which will be a merit in them when the customs are Yours). The first *culbut and foramination* after the chestnut moon must be with the senior wife, that is to say Saracca, and it must be her last enjoyment of her king (for which we later shed many pleasant tears together).

When Saracca was satisfied, and had given off her

gurgling cry, there was a great shout of 'Suruk suruk suruk' outside the palace. Apparently, on this occasion, as well as husbands being found for each of the other virgins, there is throughout the tribe a very general *culbut and foramination*, which they call 'suruk', resembling, if I judge it correctly, some lewd orgy of the emperor Nero. This is an area ripe for reform. I have it in mind, Lord.

Meanwhile Saracca fetched the monthly report, deposited it in the archive of which I thought she alone would be the keeper but which is now in the care of Noaku (my new senior wife), and returned to where I sat in my cotton throne. This time she led me not into renewed revelries with my assembled wives but towards a small private chamber off the courtyard. Understanding what must be afoot, I trembled at being about to discover my fate. Had Father John understood?

He had. Lying in a hammock, clad only in those threads at waist and wrist (so soon to be redundant), was my new-found treasure. Her pretty feet dangled on either side of the hammock, a position the girls here often adopt when resting, and her face was turned towards me. There was a smile in her eye, and round her mouth, so delicate as to be almost imperceptible. Yet for any who could perceive, it seemed to promise as much and as miraculously soon as the tight rosebud to the gardener. She did not move, except to extend an arm towards me, exposing her breasts. 'My name is Taijé,' she said.

TAIJÉ

YOU SHALL WAIT NO LONGER

[24 June 1560]

My text for today, for last month, for next month, for always: *thy Wife will be beautiful, thou wilt be kindly used by her* [lines 244–5]. Maître Rabelais, soothsayer as well as buttockstirrer and ballockmaster, you foresaw Taijé. And yet, foreseeing her, you could never see her as she is.

Two days and a night we stayed together in that inner room, while the twenty older women brought us delicacies. My wife is indeed beautiful. And I was kindly used by her. And she by me.

Taijé. Your name is like yourself being kindly used, for it starts crisp and bright with the sound TAI and then yields, moistens, melts into the soft warm welcome of JÉ. Maître Rabelais was fond of making lists and I understand now his pleasure in them. Taijé:

Hair shiny as new-split coal

Toes ten in number, *un deux trois et cetera* many times over, for we are learning French together

Eyes the best dark olives of Valmonay

Instep vulnerable, ticklish, within the hard curving rind of her sole

Ears like soft single grapes to be sucked from the vine, for only the lobes peep out below her hair (cut straight round, like a monk's grown long)

Heels hard and full of ravines for one so young, being the occasion of much sympathy and concern whenever noticed

Nose so small and soft it is impossible to believe it could not be squashed flush with the face, but try as you may it never can

Ankles my thumb and forefinger just just just go round, but we both have to concentrate

Knees but no, we must spend more time in the northern hemisphere, for though the jungle of Brazil be our destination, the Lord in His wisdom has placed more cities of note and more places of pilgrimage north of the equatorial line (once marked by cotton thread, but that was removed long before these peregrinations began in earnest)

Mouth a source of ceaseless chatter as ceaselessly stopped with kisses, though to do so is like blocking a mountain spring with a cairn of pebbles, it will bubble through in spite of all to delight you

Chin a dimple in it, and under her chin she loves, like a cat, to be stroked

Shoulders I pass them by as leading to her arms and hands, hands and arms which I feel more than see, around me, down my spine, under, through, all over

Breasts her breasts; yes

Knees she loves to be stroked and kissed behind her knees, lying face down in her hammock or on the thick cushions of soft fluffed cotton which they lay on the ground here for matrimonial purposes, which brings me to the mountain ranges just south of the equator, so infinitely intriguing to the passing traveller; turn over now

Belly plump, delectable belly, swelling uplands round a tiny primeval crater, good for kissing

Thigh smooth on the inside beyond belief, beyond the confirmation even of a thousand renewed experiments to test that soft perfection, a perfection made more perfect by its one defect, the mole like a gentle arrow which seems to point the traveller . . .

All lists must end, Maître Alcofribas Nasier [anagram of François Rabelais under which *Pantagruel* was first published], having their natural conclusion, destination, bottom line or *terminus ad quem*, and this monthly report now being sufficiently complete I am able to say, master listmaker Rabelais, enough titillation or foreplay or *going about the Bush with frivolous circumstances*, for I come now to the bottom of my leaf and to what in their own Tupinili language is called, openly and without polite evasion, Taijé's *carapua* which being translated (though I know not why) is her

ROUND POTATO

[26 July 1560]

If you have messengers at your disposal, whoever you are, send to the Sultan of Turkey and enquire whether his wives live at peace one with another. Mine do.

71

The others have been content that my thoughts are all of Taijé. And though every piece of fruit in the past three months should have been hers, by right of conquest, she insists that I attend not to her needs alone. Truth to tell, at the end of one of our pleasant games together, in which so many play with such sweet invention, I am often not certain upon whom in particular my royal favours have been bestowed. Thus are we one happy family, of whom I shall now tell you more.

The number of a king's wives here is twenty. That is to say he always has women in attendance with from fifteen to thirty-four chestnuts in their cotton bags (hidden in many secret places around the palace until the next chestnut moon). The senior wife is she who has thirty-four, and this on my arrival here was my good Saracca, who has guided me so lovingly in the traditions of my kingdom. But at the last birthday she received her thirty-fifth chestnut, reaching the age when wives leave the palace and return, with their royal children, to their own families in the town. So there was much sweet leave-taking, from myself and from the other wives, her partners here for so many years. That month – with the arrival of Taijé and the departure of Saracca – more fruit was distributed than ever before in my reign. Twenty-four pieces.

I do sometimes wonder, Lord, whether so much public service might endanger my health, and whether You instituted Christian marriage to preserve the strength of Your male subjects. But on this matter our text here is uncompromising, and it accords so well with the pre-existing notions of these savages that to disregard its wisdom would be a great affront and a dangerous folly. *Fortifie thy Nerves so strongly, that there be no discontinuance in the Knocks of the Venerian thwacking, else thou art lost, pour Soul: for if there pass long intervals betwixt the Priapising Feats, and that thou make an intermission of too large a time, that will befall thee, which betides the Nurses, if they desist from giving suck to children, they lose their Milk; and if continually thou do not hold thy Aspersory Tool in exercise, and keep thy Mentul going, thy Lactinician Nectar will be gone, and it will serve thee only as a Pipe to piss out at, and thy Cods for a Wallet of lesser value than a Beggars Scrip.* [lines 68–78]

A happy family then, though often exhausted. Twelve children by now of whom, Lord, You have taken three. They died Christians, for I baptised them myself, remembering what Maître Zwingli has written – that in the unavoidable absence of an ordained minister any Christian may administer this sacrament to infants in danger of imminent death. [I can find no trace of this passage in Zwingli.] The children have names, after our Huguenot custom, from the Old Testament, when Your chosen people, Lord, struggled against famine and pestilence, tyrant and torment, as all good Christians must.

My favourite among them is little Rebecca, my first-born daughter, who now turns her head and looks about most prettily. Her first two brothers were Samson and Isaiah. These both survive. After them there have been Jeremiah; Jonah; Elijah, I believe; and Zedekiah, I am sure of him. And among the girls Sarah, Abigail and some others. I shall know them better in years to come.

Our harmony is disturbed only by Friar John, who on

many counts tries to frustrate my royal will. *Item*, he does not wish that my wives and children shall learn French. He says that French is a language for men, and a language of special dignity and secret power which must be spoken only by those who are selected to sit with us in parliament. For men only? Tell that to the pearl of pearls! [Marguerite de Navarre, princess and poet to whom Rabelais dedicated Book III of *Gargantua and Pantagruel*, and who was known as 'marguerite des marguerites', or pearl of pearls.] But she might as well not exist where Friar John is concerned, for we have no written mention of her here and whenever it suits him he goes, as they say, only by the Book. It is always text text text with him, and he will find an apt quotation for every case.

This is the cause of another of our complaints against him, that he is always in and out of the palace, to the fury of my wives, who say that such a thing was never before known. He replies that we now have, as Sieur de la Taille promised us and as was fulfilled, a new religion of the Book. And from the Book he quotes the passage where I, Panurge, say plainly to him, Friar John, that I *shall have always by me pretty Girls clothed with the Name of my Wives Waiting-Maids*, and that they may lie under his wings and he be *Night-Protector of their Sister-hood*. From this he argues, and has several times carried in parliament, that a freedom which I have given him in writing I have no power to take away again verbally. For as it is written, so it is written.

I sometimes wish that I had suffered longer from my intestinal flux and so had used up as bumfodder all the Rabelaisian *oeuvre* instead of only ninety-nine parts of it. But Taijé shall console me. *And*, Friar John, she shall do so in her few words of French, as aptly chosen for the purpose as any of your quotations,

CON QUE TU ES

[24 August 1560]

We have had the opening of parliament. And a great deal of ceremony. If there is one thing Friar John enjoys as much as making a speech, it is featuring in a ceremony.

The occasion was planned for the full moon, to follow my customary emergence with the fruit. That event too has been turned by the Friar into an elaborate ritual. Before I appear, he leads the congregation in a chant from holy writ, rehearsing – as religious people will – the possibilities of doom while remaining inwardly confident of deliverance. Friar John calls out the French phrases from the Book and the assembled tribesmen repeat them in the manner of the *toucan*, a bird living in the jungle here which can easily be taught to speak good nonsense. It sounds, at this stage, a gloomy enough litany as I wait to make my entrance, though I have the satisfaction of knowing that my own efforts will alter their tune.

Friar John: Jaded Cod. (Crowd: JADED COD.) Friar John: Faded Cod. (Crowd: FADED COD.) And so it goes on. Mouldy Cod, MOULDY COD. Musty Cod, MUSTY COD. Foundered Cod, FOUNDERED COD. Distempered Cod, DISTEMPERED COD. Discouraged Cod,

DISCOURAGED COD. Forlorn Cod, FORLORN COD. Unsavoury Cod, UNSAVOURY COD. Seedless Cod, SEEDLESS COD. Dangling Cod, DANGLING COD. [lines 255–64]

Dangling Cod is my cue. Upon this disconsolate phrase I step forth, in refutation, with my brimming bowl of fruit. The friar leads the crowd in a great cheer. My mask is removed and he throws the first piece of fruit to the congregation, accompanying it and each successive piece with a phrase from the litany.

Friar John: Thumping Cod. (Crowd: THUMPING COD, and a scrabble for the fruit.) Bumping Cod, BUMPING COD. Tumbling Cod, TUMBLING COD. Berumpling Cod, BERUMPLING COD. I usually end around BRAWNY COD [fifteen pieces of fruit, line 3], but have reached in my time MANLY COD, SNORTING COD and even SUPERLATIVE COD [twenty-four pieces].

On this particular occasion, after the last piece of fruit had been distributed, the Friar led a procession (myself in second place, the king being preceded by his chamberlain) to the new parliament, which faces the palace. It is the tallest building in my kingdom, its palm-leaf roof sloping steeply from a fine point. The entrance is large enough to walk in without stooping, unlike the ordinary dwelling places of these savage people where a visitor must duck below the eaves to gain admittance. After a roundabout route through the town, accompanied by a large crowd and much rattling of maracas, there marched into this new building the Friar, myself and the nine other parliamentarians – in other words our entire 'French' community – leaving the *Troglodytick People* outside.

The interior had been completed since the previous new moon, when I had returned to the palace. I saw now a dais at the far end with two stools upon it. Facing it was a bench with accommodation (just) for nine. Scant furnishing for so grandiose a building, but strictly sufficient for the deliberations of this small assembly. I was installed on the right-hand stool, the Friar now for the first time on my left, after which he launched into the ritual of name-swapping which has become the custom at the start of all our gatherings.

'*My dear friend Panurge,*' he began, '*my Billy*, pray be welcome in this your new parliament.'

I knew my routine. '*My Harcabuzing Cod, and Buttock-stirring Ballock, Fryar John, my Friend*' (I do believe the reason he loves this rigmarole is that he has so many more names and titles in the Book than I, his king), '*my Metropolitan Cod, my left Ballock,*' (so *this* was why he now sat upon my left!), 'I am proud indeed that you have built for my people this new parliament and I take it upon myself to open the proceedings here by moving a vote of thanks' (if he favoured ceremony, I could play his game), 'to yourself, my first minister or Friar, my trusted *Ballockette*, and to our nine parliamentarians here, and through them also to the *Hypogastrian, lower sort of Troglodytick People*' (if he liked quoting, I could outquote him too, or so I thought) 'who by their *sempiternal labouring* have broken ground here *within the Paphian trenches*, and so have created this noble building.'

I believed myself to be indulging only in the common courtesies of parliamentary business, but apparently I had . . . The leaf ends but these are important matters and I shall memorise my words and continue next month as I began.

[23 September 1560]

I believed myself to be indulging only in the normal courtesies of parliamentary business, but I had stumbled upon the main topic of the morning. To the assembled parliament it must have seemed that the king and his first minister were well rehearsed in the manipulation of affairs, for Friar John now said:

'My dear *Billy*, I am glad indeed that you raise the matter of the *Troglodytick People*, for we must decide how best to prevent their returning to the life of *Gentlemen, idle upon their Rents and Revenues*, ensuring instead that they continue to *work for their Livelyhood*.'

It transpired that the Friar, having persuaded the men of the tribe, against their custom, to work from dawn to dusk in the building of this parliament house, was eager that they should not revert to their old ways. He proposed that they should now provide furnishings suitable for the dignity of the building, being encouraged to do so by pride in their achievement thus far and by the threat of nameless punishments specified in the new religion (the precise details of such punishments to be derived from further intense study of the Book).

Such a scheme for the employment of the common people met with the approval of all, and this first session of parliament seemed about to drift without further ado

78

into our normal morning business together (analysis of specific passages of the Book, for the entire text is already memorised by all ten, followed by an advanced French lesson). I suddenly saw, Lord, a chance to further our true end, Yours and mine, for yes, it is still assuredly Ours.

I proposed that the proceedings in parliament should never formally end without a discussion of religion, the highest topic known to man, and of that Truth which has been revealed or can be sensed *beyond* the ten pages of the Book itself. The Friar looked displeased, caring for nothing beyond the Book. But I persisted. For I had seen, in these new surroundings, a subtle way forward. By analogy.

'I am your king,' I began. None could dissent from this. 'But I also have a King, one who is greater than I.' By this easy path, conformable to their own savage notions, I planned to tell them, Lord, of Your power and mercy and saving grace. 'The word of my King is absolute,' I said. 'His Will is greater than mine. Wherever He beckons I must follow. And His name is Jesus Christ.'

During this speech, to my surprise, Friar John had been staring at me with a light of recognition and joy in his eye. At last, I thought, Your Will shall be done. But on the mention of Your holy Name his expression changed.

'*By Saint Rigomer* I know this King, for he is in the Book,' he said, 'and I understand at last what *my dear friend Panurge* has been talking about when he speaks of a greater *Cod* . . . '

'God,' I said, but he went on regardless.

79

' . . . an even more *Superlative Cod* who is above him and who is his King. For this King is in the Book, but his name is not Jesus Christ. It is *Pantagruel.*'

This was a preposterous error, easy enough one would think to correct, too ridiculous, but the Friar was ready as ever with chapter and verse. '*The thing that I have greatest reason to dread is some long absence of our King Pantagruel (to whom I must needs bear Company, should he go to all the Devils of Barathrum).*' [lines 233–6]

'Tell us more,' said the Friar, seeming now like a novice in a seminary, 'tell us more of *Pantagruel*, and of the wicked *Devils of Barathrum*, for we must delve into every secret of the Book.' The nine nonentities nodded their approval and sang out, 'Tell us more of *Pantagruel*, the *Superlative Cod of Cods*,' for they never disagree with Friar John.

And so, Lord, a dilemma. I had been about to tell them of You, and of how You triumph for our sake over the Devil (of *Barathrum* if need be), and for the first time these savage people, the ten most influential in their tribe, were eager to hear. But they were determined to attach to You the name of a foolish heathen giant hatched in scurrility by a fornicating monk. Such a name for Your Person? It seemed out of the question, until it occurred to me by how many names You already encourage us to know You: Alpha and Omega, Jehovah, Yahweh, the Ineffable, God Almighty, Jesus Christ, the Holy Ghost, the Trinity, Three-in-One and One-in-Three, the Lord of Hosts and a host of Lords. If the underlying truth is there, for that is the essential matter, might not even a name such as Pantagruel slip into the list on a temporary basis without lasting damage?

I decided that it might. And for the first time, with their absolute attention, I was able to tell these young savages how Pantagruel grew up, the son of a carpenter in distant Palestine, and how he so attended to his studies that he was able even as a child to dispute with the elders in the Temple, and of his baptism in the Jordan and his saving ministry – many many details I told them, You know them, Lord – ending with the good news that if they followed this King, my Lord and their Lord (*'Pantagruel, Pantagruel,'* they shouted, and their enthusiasm was unmistakable, even though on the surface misplaced), they would all be saved and have a place in Paradise.

'I thank you, *Billy,*' said the Friar in conclusion, 'for expounding so ably this other *Ergo.*'

'Ergo?' said I. 'Ergo what?'

'The other *Ergo,*' he replied, 'from the concluding paragraph of the Book.'

The Book. I saw now that he wore his sanctimonious quoting face.

'Oh?' I said, giving nothing away but still not seeing how I had inadvertently strayed back to Rabelais.

'*And finally with this other Ergo* . . . ' Friar John had turned towards the assembled members of parliament as if conducting them in one of our recital sessions, and they joined with him in full voice: ' . . . *thou shalt be saved, and have a place in Paradise.*' [lines 247–8]

True words indeed, if only we can rightly anchor them.

[22 October 1560]

Does nothing change? I live in rags (for my breeches and shirt fall now to pieces), eating root flour in place of good porridge, speaking Tupinili for half the month with twenty naked women and garbled French the other half with ten naked youths – evidence surely that the person and life of this Jacques le Balleur is very different from the solemn Huguenot of two years ago. And yet, as we argue this *Ergo* and that in parliament, debating whether *all the Devils* are still in their home territory of *Barathrum* or are spread now throughout the world, I am reminded of just such discussions in Fort Coligny.

If you have doubted any part of what I tell you, reader, find some poor cleric and send him to the archives in Paris to search and copy for you. There he will surely discover the report which the Chevalier de Villegagnon sent back in the *Rosée* with one of our ministers, Guillaume Chartier, telling of our arguments over the Holy Sacrament and seeking the guidance of Admiral Coligny.

The trouble began one warm evening about a week before our first Pentecost in Antarctic France. The three ministers were dining that day with the governor of our little community, the Chevalier de Villegagnon, and they were discussing how we would improve, educate, civilise the savage Americans who are the original inhabitants of this great new world.

'The first improvement to be made', said Maître Pierre Richier, the oldest of our three ministers, 'is to end their abominable custom of eating one another.'

This is a custom now known after themselves as

cannibalism, for our Christian explorers first came upon
this practice among the people dwelling in the Canib
islands. [In fact among the Caribs of the Caribbean,
incorrectly transcribed as 'Canib' by Columbus through
reliance on the Arawak dialect.] All agreed that this must
be a priority, alongside the spreading of the good news
of Yourself, Lord, and of Your promise to mankind
through Your death and resurrection.

It was at this point that Villegagnon said we must
tread carefully in presenting this double message of
prohibition and promise.

'Oh?' said Richier. 'Why?'

'Lest the minds of some, whether simple or cynical,
detect a similarity between what we proscribe and what
we prescribe.'

If any of the three ministers foresaw the heresy that
was about to be uttered, they held their peace.

'In what way?' asked Richier.

'In the eating of human flesh,' came the reply.

Their pulses quickened, but still they stared at him in
silence. (I am not making this up about the pulses, in
the way that Maître Rabelais might when spinning his
fantastic tales, for I had all the details of this encounter
from the lips of Antoine de la Taille himself, the very
lips which confront me now in shrunken form as I
write. The pulse of Sieur de la Taille quickened, and as
all pulses and all true ministers are much the same, I say
their pulses quickened.) But still they said nothing by
way of protest, for they wished heresy to stand
revealed beyond dispute or dissembling, in its naked
deformity.

'I am sorry,' said Maître Richier, for the Chevalier

seemed disinclined to continue, 'but I do not see the link.'

'It is one of seeming substance, though not of essence,' said Villegagnon (his very choice of words revealing him for the quibbling heretic pedant that he was), 'in the parallel between flesh and blood at these savage festivities in the mouths of cannibals, and flesh and blood at the Mass . . . '

'Holy Communion!' shrieked Guillaume Chartier.

'Quiet!' interjected Richier, seeming on the surface more impatient with friend than foe. 'Go on.'

' . . . in the mouths of Christians.'

'What flesh and blood?'

'The flesh and blood of our beloved Jesus Christ, Who died for our sakes and rose on the third day, and Who offers Himself to us in the sacrament of Holy Communion.'

Now at last Richier revealed himself, bringing his fist down with a crash on the table.

'You betray the name of that same Jesus Christ,' he thundered at Villegagnon, 'and you betray us, His followers. You wear our clothes,' (for he was sober-suited as any Geneva citizen), 'you ape our customs,' (he ate like us, modestly, with his hat on), 'you kneel at our devotions,' (as indeed he did, seeming-devoutly, at morning prayers), 'and all the time beneath your serge there lurks the black heart of an unreformed papist. You live here like a whore in a convent. You live here like a cuckoo in a nest.'

Maître Richier concluded with one or other of these powerful similes, but almost certainly not with both. However, when describing this important scene on later occasions, my friend Sieur de la Taille sometimes said one, sometimes the other. To be certain of accuracy I include here both the cuckoo and the whore.

Which brings me to the bottom of my leaf and to the happy thought that I have a convent of my own with twenty in the order, some of them far from novices. Strange times for an old monk, as Maître Luther used to say with his nun and his children at Wittenberg. But these are important matters, and you shall hear more of them.

[21 November 1560]

'Fetch me the Bible.'

Villegagnon sent his page to the chamber where he slept, and turned again to Richier, Chartier and de la Taille.

'I take it that you are of my opinion, gentlemen, for which I am indebted to Maître Calvin and other leaders of the reform, that all truth is in the Bible? That is why Holy Scripture has now been translated into the vulgar tongues, so that we may receive God's word without the obscurities of Latin grammar or the need for Roman interpreters. On this point we may surely agree, that the Bible cannot lie?'

'If rightly interpreted,' said Richier.

The page returned and placed the Bible before Villegagnon. He was a learned man, this governor of ours, in his deceitful way, and it took him little time to find his text.

'I draw your attention', he said, 'to the Gospel according to St Matthew.' Forgive me, Lord, I forget the chapter and verse, but he gave it in the approved manner [26:26], and read out his text. 'Jesus took bread and said, "Take, eat; this is my body."'

Villegagnon closed the Book reverently, well pleased with himself, and leant back in his chair. '"Take, eat; this is my body." Where is the ambiguity in that? And later: "Drink, this is my blood, which is shed for many." Flesh and blood. What say you to that? Do you call our Lord a liar?'

Richier reached for the Book and drew it towards him. As a minister he found his way to his text even sooner than Villegagnon. 'From the Gospel of St John, "Whoever eats my flesh and drinks my blood has eternal life" and then in explanation "The spirit gives life, not the flesh".' [6:54 and 63] Richier closed the Bible and pushed it back to Villegagnon, as if no further discussion were needed.

Villegagnon said that this verse from John was true, very true, for the Holy Spirit does indeed give life, being with the flesh and blood of Jesus Christ in the unleavened bread. 'How otherwise would St John have said that the spirit gives life, not the flesh, if the flesh were not also present? – As one might say of a salad dressing that the vinegar gives the sharp taste, not the oil, but no man would say this if the dressing did not indeed contain both oil and vinegar.'

It was Maître Chartier who now dismissed this seeming-fair argument with a homily upon the temptations of the false analogy, likening it to the snake in the Garden of Eden, so convincing at first sight but found, when seen with deeper understanding, to be both wrong and dangerous.

Then Maître Richier expounded the doctrine of the transferred metaphor, often used in the scriptures, whereby the symbol is identified by the name of the thing symbolised. Thus when Jesus said, 'Take, eat; this is my body', He was not handing the disciples His body, He was handing them bread. He certainly did not mean them there and then to eat His body (which, as Sieur de la Taille later expounded it, mocking this papistical nonsense of transubstantiation, would have resulted in a very different Last Supper and would have frustrated our salvation, making impossible, for lack of a body, both the Crucifixion and the Resurrection). Our Lord meant only that they should eat the bread, the very bread which He was handing them, which he appointed to symbolise His body.

'Then why', asked Villegagnon, 'did He not say, Take, eat; this symbolises My body? He said, Take, eat; this *is* my body. Is, is, is. There can be no two ways.'

At this Antoine de la Taille, who had not yet spoken (controlling with difficulty his fiery temper), at last burst out: 'So all these years, Monsieur le Chevalier, you have been eating the real flesh and blood of our Saviour in your cannibal Masses. What does it taste like, human flesh?'

'You blaspheme,' said Villegagnon, angry in his turn.

'How blaspheme? The flesh and blood must be from the human part of our Lord, and if corporeally present in the bread it surely has a taste. To me, you must understand, the blessed Sacrament tastes only of bread. And this blood you drink, is it salty?'

'Enough,' said Richier. 'You are to keep the discussion on the level appropriate to theology. But tell me, Chevalier, when does the change occur, in your opinion, from bread to flesh?'

'When the priest — or minister — lays his hand upon the bread and speaks the words of our Lord, "This is my body, which is given for you." I come back always to the Gospel.'

'And at that moment the bread changes to flesh?'

'Indeed.'

'Entirely?'

'How else?'

'The Lutherans say it becomes then bread *and* flesh, the flesh existing in, with and under the bread.'

'A skin of bread to explain the appearance? That is too literal. The sacrament is a mystery. We need not attempt to explain it.'

'It is you who are literal, insisting on, "Take, eat; this is my body."'

'I do insist. These are the words of our Lord at the height of His ministry, when He instituted the most holy sacrament of Communion. At such a moment my soul dares not disbelieve Him, nor accuse Him of equivocation. Your souls are your own affair. You may disbelieve Him as you will.'

'Disbelieve Him!' Again de la Taille's anger brimmed over and now he was on his feet. 'Interpret Him as He would we should, you should rather say. Our beloved Lord said many deep things which heathens like yourself, stewed in your own sweet pride, may make to seem contradictory, which is why such profound sayings need the services of trained ministers to expound them.'

'Calm down,' said Richier, 'and sit down.' But de la Taille would not.

'Trained ministers?' said Villegagnon. 'I have heard much talk in reformed circles of the priesthood of all believers, each man finding God for himself in the Book.'

'Believers, indeed you have it,' shouted de la Taille, 'not cannibals, foaming red at the mouth before the Communion table . . . '

At this point he was carried off to spend the night in the half-completed fort. None of the three ministers had noticed that when de la Taille first lost his temper the little page, on a sign from Villegagnon, had slipped away to fetch soldiers.

Theology in this modern age is a violent matter, and that night saw the start of our own small wars of religion.

[20 December 1560]

I have been thinking all month about Sieur de la Taille. While describing his abuse of the heretic Villegagnon and his night in the fortress dungeon, I was reminded most forcibly of this man's difficult temper. How absolute he was in his judgements, how swift and unyielding in his decisions. He had a large heavy face, with a black beard, and eyebrows that jutted forward above glinting eyes as if to butt one in the forehead when he was making an assertion.

Did this temper cause his death among these friendly people? Searching for an answer I stare at the shrivelled head on the rack here, but there is no link, beyond the first shudder of recognition, between this shrunken object and the man I knew. You might as well look for hints of the plum among the wrinkles of the prune. I must give up inspecting him.

But I get no clues either from Friar John, or from Noaku and my other wives who were also his. Why not? There is some mystery here. How did he die?, I ask. Suddenly. Suddenly, yes, but from what? From a disease? Yes. What sort of disease? An incapacitating disease. Incapacitating? In what way incapacitating? Could he not walk? Oh, he could walk. Was he blind? No, he could see. And so it goes on. A disease, it seems, for which they do not know the cause and of which they cannot describe the symptoms.

I have come to believe they must have murdered him. But why? And after making him their king? Does that mean danger for me, who have received nothing but friendliness from these people? (Apart from the frust-rations put in my path by Friar John.) Or was the cause in Sieur de la Taille himself? I cannot help staring once more into the puckered hollows that were his eyes, seeking to know whether the choler which landed him in gaol on Fort Coligny also brought about his death here.

When de la Taille was released from his dungeon, about the time of Pentecost some years ago, those of us in the reformed party gathered in a quiet corner at one end of the island. It was a council of war except that we were few and unarmed, no match for Villegagnon's soldiers. The question was only whether to submit or to go our own way. Maîtres Richier and Chartier were for diplomacy. The Chevalier, they said, was a powerful nobleman long steeped in the papistical heresy who had only recently seen the light. Time would be needed to clear out every dark corner in the soul of such a man. They believed that his heart was for reform, and in evidence they revealed that after the arrest of de la Taille he had promised to send Chartier back in the *Rosée* with letters for the admiral and for Maître Calvin about our differences. De la Taille would have none of this, branding it a ploy to deprive us of one of our ministers and maintaining that the sealed letters would contain secret messages to our disadvantage. [Strangely, this anticipates a later rumour among Huguenots in France that Villegagnon had sent Chartier home bearing orders for his own arrest, though there is no evidence that he was arrested. He sailed in the *Rosée* on 4 June 1557.]

De la Taille proposed instead that we should leave Fort Coligny and establish our own reformed mission on the mainland. The savages on this part of the coast had been found to be friendly (they hated and feared the Portuguese, and so did we), and we might therefore without too great danger move among them to spread the Word of the Lord. We would also be well placed to strike inland, where there were reports of vast quantities of gold (gold being a useful commodity to speed up the propagation of the gospel). So said de la Taille that morning, and I for one believed that he spoke well, as did my friend the tailor, André Lafon, and Oyster John, with Nicolas Raviquet and Jean du Bordel.

And so it was that while Maître Richier, advising caution and compromise, remained on the island with most of our party from Geneva, we five loaded a boat with provisions for a few days and with a supply of the cheap Honfleur cutlery and buckles and beads which these savage people take for great riches, accepting them as recompense for much hospitality.

We rowed ourselves across to the mainland with our own fiery minister in the stern, his Bible upon his knees and his hair unkempt still from his night's lodging. As we bent to the oars he encouraged us with passages from the Acts of the Apostles, telling how Barnabas and Paul sailed to Cyprus and how the Lord struck blind a sorcerer who opposed them. Sieur de la Taille bellowed out these comforting words in a voice which rang with enthusiasm above the roar of the waves.

[From this passage in the Authorised Version one can well imagine the pugnacious minister making the most of the fate which befalls the enemies of righteousness. Acts 13: 7–12: 'The deputy of the country, Sergius Paulus, a prudent man, called for Barnabas and Saul, and desired to hear the word of God. But Elymas the sorcerer withstood them, seeking to turn away the deputy from the faith. Then Saul, (who also is called Paul,) filled with the Holy Ghost, set his eyes on him, and said, "O full of all subtilty and mischief, thou child of the devil, thou enemy of all righteousness, wilt thou not cease to pervert the right ways of the Lord? And now, behold, the hand of the Lord is upon thee, and thou shalt be blind, not seeing the sun for a season." And immediately there fell on him a mist and a darkness; and he went about seeking some to lead him by the hand. Then the deputy, when he saw what was done, believed, being astonished at the doctrine of the Lord.']

I shall not tell here how Oyster John was offered, with profound courtesy and much ceremony, the forearm of a child, for I am cramped now for space and have left to the end the real news. Taijé is with child, or, as she herself now loves to say,

ENCEINTE

1561

[19 January]

We rowed up the coast of the bay until we found a suitable place for our first night's settlement, a clearing by the mouth of a small stream. We expected the savages to find us here and to lead us to their place of habitation, for when a ship first makes landfall from France the shore is always crowded with curious Americans even before the boats are within hailing distance. But it seems our small craft had approached unobserved. The following morning we hid it as best we could beneath a fallen tree by the stream's edge and struck inland, in search of those whom Sieur de la Taille seemed confident of converting at a stroke to the reformed religion but whose acquaintance the rest of us, mere carpenters or tailors, anticipated with greater apprehension.

It was early evening before we came upon an encampment of the savages. In that part of Antarctic France their dwelling places are more like fortresses than villages, for the houses are packed tight within a high palisade of wooden staves, leaving not a chink between them except for the entrance. Each fenced-in place of this kind sits in the middle of a clearing in the jungle, and is the home of one tribe or clan.

The paths leading to any settlement are made difficult and slow of passage by great tendrils hanging from the trees. Nearby there lurk unseen spies, whose task was made easy in this case by Sieur de la Taille's habit of vigorous hymn-singing as we hacked our way through the jungle. As a result, when we stumbled suddenly into a wide clearing, we found the chief and his most important counsellors sitting outside their palisade to greet us. The nature of that greeting would depend on the answer to a question, for which luckily we were prepared.

'Ferranghi? Ferransay?'

'Ferranghi' is what they call the Portuguese [the reason seems obscure], but we had been assured that the answer 'Français' would earn us a warm welcome in these parts. And so it proved. With smiles and friendly thumps on the back we were motioned to sit in a row on the ground, facing the chief. When we were settled, or almost settled (the savages dispose of their legs on these occasions in a manner not easily discovered by ourselves), a joint of cold meat was produced. It was made plain that we should each take a bite and pass it on, in the manner of a loving cup at home. Oyster John was on the right and was the first to receive the offering. He had it already to his lips when there was a shout of 'Stop!' from Sieur de la Taille. 'Pass it to me,' he thundered. He gave one glance at the meat in his hand and resumed his bellowing, about an abomination in the sight of the Lord and a running sore of blasphemy, while seeming on the point of either flinging the offending morsel upon the ground or even assaulting with it our host, the savage chief. I sat beside de la Taille, and felt it politic to restrain him, murmuring that we were six against several hundred, and taking from him the blasphemous limb.

The chief resolved the matter, signing to an attendant, who relieved me of the unfortunate child's arm. I was pleased to see that the chief was still all smiles, and the others took their cue from him. Maybe they knew already that we French do not share their perverted taste for human flesh, and so were determined not to allow the behaviour of our man of God to spoil the ceremony of friendship.

Another delicacy was produced for us, recognisable at a glance as the leg of a very large chicken which lives in Antarctic France [presumably a relative of the turkey, found by the conquistadors in North America]. While Oyster John took a bite of this leg, one of their party sank his teeth in corresponding fashion into the roasted arm, and so the two joints were passed from hand to hand and mouth to mouth, back and forth among us, until each was finished and the laws of hospitality had been fulfilled.

[17 February 1561]

We spent several months with Kuatu and his people, and learnt much about the ways and notions of the savage Americans. They regard war as a natural state of affairs between themselves and the neighbouring tribes, but this constant struggle is not, as with us at home, about important matters.

In Christendom powerful lords march on their enemies, and brave men die, to decide the great principles by which we may live in peace and virtue, as for example whether there are two or seven sacraments and whether the wine shall be given along with the bread. As soon as all blasphemous errors, the cause of these conflicts, have been eradicated, there will be no more war.

With us, therefore, the purpose of war is peace. It is very different among these savages. Here every war creates the next, because the winning side captures prisoners in the skirmish whom they take back to their own village. There, amid much ceremony and self-congratulation, they eat them. Thus the losing side is offered a grievous affront, requiring vengeance, and so it goes on.

Such an affront may be given at any time, for the victors do not necessarily consume all their prisoners at the victory feast. Some they keep alive, treating them as honoured guests, providing them with a wife, a house and the means of life. They encourage in this way the development of a family. Later, when for reasons of state they wish to offend once more the neighbouring tribe, they will eat their captive and his children with him (not his wife, for she is one of their own). Just such an emblem of state was the arm offered to Oyster John, for it belonged to the child of a man captured previously and pampered ever since – though only perhaps as a peasant pampers his best goat, living proof that his table will be better graced than his neighbour's.

In a similar plight is the unfortunate Ramram Ghi, a prisoner from another tribe now living in our village here. He was captured, I would guess, three years ago. He has been given a pretty wife (just one), and has a male child a little older than my Rebecca. Like me, he is both captive and honoured guest. Like me, he receives from his captors many kindnesses. Like me, he is often the central character in village ceremonies – except that his, light-hearted though they seem, have the bitter flavour of a game which may suddenly become real.

Accompanied by much laughter and merriment Ramram Ghi must from time to time dance among us, calling out, 'I, your food, have come' (we gnash our teeth), 'I, your food, dance among you to whet your appetite' (gnash, gnash), and then he will boast how many of our people he has eaten and how tasty we were (even if this is not true, even if he has eaten nobody at all, he must make this boast, for he has his own pride to consider), and we gnash our teeth more furiously.

Then Friar John will feel the arms and legs of Ramram Ghi (I have refused to do so, Lord, although their king), and will declare that he needs fattening; we shall eat him later; meanwhile bring him food; bring us all food. So once again we feast with him, and with his wife and child, on pig or chicken, all the while making plain that the greater delicacy sits among us. I am working to save him, Lord.

This was surely another reason why they found the Book of Maître Rabelais so very much to their liking, and therefore self-evidently true. *No Malefactor shall be executed who shall not, for a day or two at least before, be permitted to culbut and foraminate; he will perhaps therewith beget a Male.* What malefactor greater than he who boasted of having eaten their aunt or cousin? And had they not provided Ramram Ghi with a pretty partner in *foramination* for months and years, let alone a day or two? And had he not begotten a male? A prophetic Book indeed.

My stay with Kuatu's people enabled me to learn much of the Tupinamba language, very similar to the

Tupinili which we speak here and therefore of great assistance to me in my mission. I discovered also how to inhale the smoke which they derive from burning leaves, the same kind of leaf that I write on now, which they suck into their lungs through narrow tubes. At first our people were doubtful about this strange custom, until Oyster John said that if it proved harmful we could always give it up. I now derive much pleasure from it, forming as it does an important part of our ceremonies in parliament.

Every day, while we stayed with Kuatu, Sieur de la Taille expounded to the ignorant Americans the message of the Bible, reading passages which we translated with the help of a savage who had worked for a while in Fort Coligny. And we were able to assist them in many practical ways. I had my joiner's tools with me, for example, the sharpness and strength of which astonished them all.

With the education of these people advancing on all fronts but one [presumably cannibalism], it seemed that a reformed settlement in Antarctic France would indeed become a reality, until one day soldiers appeared in the village. Villegagnon had found our boat, hidden at the mouth of the stream, and had sent these men to search for us. Against their muskets there was no arguing. But, as we were about to leave for the coast, Sieur de la Taille slipped away into the jungle. He had only the clothes he was wearing, for even his beloved Bible was in our baggage. The soldiers searched everywhere, staying on in the village for several days, because Villegagnon had above all specified the capture of the minister. But there was no sign of him, and we assumed he must be dead –

until, a year later, I received his message. But that is another part of the story.

[19 March 1561]

My new love is Rachel. She came into my life this past month. From the depth of my heart I thank You for her, Lord.

After my usual arousal at the stake, four weeks ago, and the first rapid *foramination* (my thoughts were elsewhere), they took me to Taijé in the small room where first we met. She lay in the hammock, much as on that occasion, her head turned towards the door, awaiting me, anticipating my approval. At her breast was this tiny perfect little creature. A child suckled by a child, for Taijé is only fifteen. I have called her Rachel, knowing that when she is older many a man will happily labour twice seven years (almost the age of Taijé herself) to win such a beauty.

We have baptised her, healthy though she is, for I do not now expect any ordained minister to lay hands on my children here. After the naming of Rachel I formally christened all my other children (twelve living now), and then in glorious unison my twenty wives and I recited Your prayer, Lord. Our Father, which art in heaven. Hallowed be Thy name. Thy kingdom come.

I make bold now to believe that it is indeed coming, in small measure, in this, my own humble kingdom. It is among the women of my family that Thy will is most nearly done. For though they repeat only the sounds of the French, they begin to learn also what those sounds must signify. In our catechism, when we are exhausted after our *Priapising Feats*, I explain to them each phrase. Already they look forward with inexpressible joy, as all Christians must, to the coming of Thy kingdom.

I have taught them to make their own confession, so that they understand what they have left undone which they ought to have done and what they have done which they ought not to have done, always excepting the *delights of Venery* within their *Aphrodisian Tennis-Court*, which would be counted in Geneva a thing many times done which ought not to have been done at all. But these girls are married, according to their own understanding, and each of them contrives *the double backed* or *two bellied beast* with none but her husband, myself. They, Lord, are surely monogamous, even if I cannot claim as much for myself. Taijé is innocent, and Rachel born in wedlock.

None of this pleases Friar John. He came into the palace, insisting as usual on his right of entry as *Night Protector of their Sister-hood*, while we were reciting Your prayer. Immediately he became abusive on two counts: that my wives were reciting in French, and that the prayer appeared nowhere in the Book of Pantagruel. I said, as I so often must here, that not *all* truth is in that wretched Book. 'Our Father, which art in heaven,' repeated Friar John, 'Thy kingdom come. This father in heaven with a kingdom, he is King Pantagruel?' I knew that he would accept Your prayer if the blessed name of Pantagruel were linked with it. Of such small steps is progress made.

'Yes,' I said.

Then the Friar sat with us and learnt the prayer himself, seeming very pleased with it (indeed it does ask pleasant favours for whoever prays), except for one phrase which he always omitted. 'As we forgive them that trespass against us.' He could see no benefit in that.

As to women learning French, Friar John returned to his old theme and would not budge. This was to be the language of parliament alone. He accepted that the prayer itself might be in French, that being the language of King Pantagruel to whom the words are addressed, but he checked that my wives learnt only the sound and not the meaning. He said to them in French, 'Shall we drink some manioc beer?' and, 'Which of these children belongs to which?', whereupon they smiled at him with such puzzled expressions as easily proved the point.

Except Taijé. Except beautiful Taijé, too quick and fiery for prudence. She replied to him in French. 'This child is mine. We have christened her Rachel, for Rachel was so beautiful that Jacob loved her fourteen years before he even fucked her. And as to manioc beer, perhaps parliament should send some as a gift to the royal palace?'

I was proud, Lord, of how much my beautiful wife has learnt in less than a year. But it was not wise.

[17 April 1561]

A month ago we all became one year older. It was chestnut time again, and I have added another wife to my collection. A pretty enough child, to whom Taijé has been most kind (even promising to teach her French!). They tell me her name is Beiju.

After my final official *foramination* with Noaku [see 28 May 1560, p. 67] I heard again the great cry outside, 'Suruk suruk suruk', and knew that the *Troglodytick People* were setting upon the *pretty little Girls that were there* (all those left unchosen by me, their king) in an *exorbitant Temptation of Lust*. This later gave me the idea which I believe, Lord, will contribute greatly to the spread of Your fame among these savages.

Friar John has complained in recent weeks that the *Troglodytick People* are becoming slack in their *sempiternal labouring*, showing an inclination towards their old ways, when they used to live like *Gentlemen, idle upon their Rents and Revenues*. Under instruction from their king (where ever before was there a joiner-monarch?) the troglodytes have made suitable furniture for the parliament house, and in recent weeks have been weaving a great carpet for the floor, since Friar John believes it improper that affairs of state should be discussed with plain earth underfoot. The weaving is done with dried fronds from their jungle trees, and pleasant patterns are made possible by the different colour and thickness of leaves. But it is slow work. And among the troglodytes collecting the leaves, drying and preparing them, or squatting round the great carpet itself, there have been mutterings.

Friar John's solution, as expounded by him in parliament, is a simple one. We must eat our prisoner. Ramram Ghi, he argues, is fat. We have fed him well. We have given him a wife, enabling him to *beget a Male* to amplify our feast. He has been heard to boast, this Ramram Ghi, of how many of our cousins and uncles he has eaten among his own people. Clearly the dissatisfaction of the troglodytes, the Friar maintains, must derive from this affront, that an avowed enemy walks freely among us and does not work (for he is treated as a privileged guest and, besides, his fingers would defile the great parliamentary carpet). This captive of ours, continues the remorseless Friar, flaunts the very plumpness which is the outward sign of our generosity towards his people, a generosity so often in the past betrayed and now betrayed once more in him, eater of our flesh.

'It is a matter of pride,' insisted Friar John, thumping the new parliament table recently provided by the troglodytes under my guidance. 'It is a matter of pride. He must be eaten.' He added that the long period of preparation for the ceremonial feast would excite and unite the whole tribe, as it invariably has done in the past, and that it would reconcile the troglodytes to their unaccustomed labours.

I have much sympathy, Lord, with this Ramram Ghi. Like me he is on his own, far from his people and with little prospect of returning home. I am more fortunate than him only in that I am a king, that I have the first place in parliament, that I have twenty wives to his one, and that there are no plans to eat me.

Of all the vices of the Americans, it is this sin of cannibalism which we Christians have most strongly determined to end. I have always attempted to protect Ramram Ghi and at that moment, in parliament a week ago, I had an idea which will save him and at the same time spread the good news, Lord, of Yourself. What, I asked myself, is even more attractive to these savages than the eating of human flesh? And, in a flash of inspiration, the answer came. *Culbut and foramination.*

To carry the vote in parliament one must work by the Book, and here Maître Rabelais came to my aid. 'Where', I asked, 'is there any mention in the Book of eating human flesh?'

The Friar was immediately on his feet. '*The Blood of a Hog's-pudding*', he said, 'that refers to Ramram Ghi, for his people are swine indeed.'

But I could outface him with the context. '*By the Blood of a Hog's-pudding*, says the Book, *till when wouldst thou delay the acting of a Husband's part?* [Lines 30–1] Do you propose the *acting of a Husband's part* after such a *Hog's-pudding?*' For I knew that in their savage customs cannibalism and *foramination* must never be combined in the same celebration, each being holy, and rival gods never willingly sharing an altar.

The members of parliament nodded approval of my argument. Friar John glowered. Then I clinched the matter.

'On the other hand the Book does describe a holy festivity which would satisfy the *Troglodytick People*,' and I recited the passage, well known to all of them, so well known that they joined with me in the recital, about the representation of the Passion at Saint Mexents. (I have not space to repeat it here, but it will be found in Maître Rabelais.)

[*I swear to thee, that many times heretofore I have perceived, and found in my Codpiece a certain kind of Energy, or efficacious Vertue, much more irregular, and of a greater Anomaly, than what I have related: I will only tell thee, that*

*once at the Representation of the Passion, which was acted at
Saint Mexents, I had no sooner entered within the Pit of the
Theater, but that forthwith, by the vertue and occult property of
it, on a sudden all that were there, both Players and Spectators,
did fall into such an exorbitant Temptation of Lust, that there
was not Angel, Man, Devil, or Deviless, upon the place, who
would not then have Bricollitched it with all their Heart and
Soul.*

*The Prompter forsook his Copy, the Devils issued out of
Hell, and carried along with them most of the pretty little Girls
that were there; yea, Lucifer got out of his Fetters.* (lines
171–85)]

'Rather than eat Ramram Ghi,' said I, 'why do we not
arrange a *Representation of the Passion*? For I can show you
how.'

And I thought with joy, as I said those words, how I
would put into this mystery play (to become an annual
event) all the truth of Your message, Lord. My heart
exulted at this new turn in my ministry, unworthy as I
have been till now.

In a parliament confronted with the *exorbitant Temptation of Lust* the vote was a formality. Eight in favour
of the Passion, only two against – Friar John and a
sour-faced boy, Pihun, who is like a shadow to the
Friar, always at his side but never between him and the
sun.

[17 May 1561]

Am I dying? Have You summoned me, Lord? I am a volcano, erupting in every direction, not knowing at any moment whether vomit or excrement will demand priority.

I repent of everything. Lord, You keep the tally. Whatever is marked against me, I accept the charge and do most heartily repent. Mercy, Lord. You give me a foretaste, raging within me, of the flames of Hell. I take Your merciful hint. Courage was never my foremost virtue. For my justification I rely only on my unshakable faith (which may from time to time have changed colour, but only on the surface) and on Your unerring Mercy.

My earthly comfort now, and another sign of Your mercy, is that You have visited upon me this grievous affliction when I can look forward, not to long sessions of quotation in parliament, but to the gently ministering arms of Taijé.

It is done. The end has come.

[It is plain from the context that Jacques is speaking not in eschatological terms but only of the end of this month's leaf. In one of his very few contributions that can be called 'editorial' in the true sense, my predecessor Luis Agostinho da Caminha tells us that 'the writing in this monthly report is uncharacteristically large, filling the entire leaf with very few words'. Clearly Jacques had come to accept the Tupinili belief that natural disturbance would follow if the entire leaf were not filled with writing. It may be observed that all men, sensing the approach of death, become reluctant to offend against any religious tenet or superstition.]

[15 June 1561]

I am not safe. I have learnt such things about my tenure as make the life of Ramram Ghi seem a model of security. The first is poison. Ramram, if he goes, will be eaten with a fanfare of trumpets, no mistaking the end or its approach. But I may shuffle off, it seems, at any moment, with a furnace in the belly and turmoil at either end.

The second discovery concerns the *Aphrodisian Tennis-Court*. Ramram goes to it, with his courtesy wife, with no peril other than providing side-dishes at his final feast. Whereas I, I now discover, foraminate for my life, the very continuance of which depends upon my *Testiculatory Ability* and *Priapaean Prowess*.

Last month, close to death from my inward up-heavals, I staggered out from the door of this sanctuary, eager only for the soothing care of Taijé but without even the strength to replace the mask on my head. Cries of horror at the sight of me from my waiting wives – not at my evident weakness, it seemed, but because my face was exposed. They fetched the mask and forced it on me, then led me as usual to the stake in spite of my protests that I was in no condition for the *Delights of Venery*. Their lascivious hands, so effective at other times, caused only revulsion. It was *Jaded Cod, Faded Cod, Mouldy Cod, Musty Cod* and so it would remain, as I told my attendant harpies, unless they could still this other fire raging within me. In my present state, I warned them, there was no chance of *tossing my sinewy*

Piece of Generation even once in the *Act of Carnal Concupiscence*, let alone *threescore and ten times in the space of Four and twenty hours.*

At this my wives went into howls of lamentation. It may perhaps be true, as the Book says, that *the Lechery of a Woman is ravenous* and that her *thing cannot be satiated*, but this selfish display even on Taijé's part (for she was the leader of their lament) while I, her lord and master, was near to death, seemed to me unreasonable. I said so in forceful terms, and I demanded to be unbound and laid on a sick bed.

This small favour, after much whispered consultation among themselves, my wives granted me; and I found myself once again in the small room, with Taijé as my nurse. There she told me the alarming truth behind these strange events.

The concern of my wives was not for themselves but for me. Taijé explained to me a most savage custom which these people have with regard to their king. I had not been told earlier, she said, because I had always proved exemplary in the performance of my royal duties. But the hard truth of the matter is that they put so much faith in the *Priapaean Prowess* of their monarch (seeing him truly as a *fabulous Fornicator*, and believing that from his good example as a *Superlative Cod* the moon waxes strong and the manioc root swells and stiffens) that if he, the king, fails in this primal duty, perforce they must change him for a better. The old king, or *Enfeebled Cod* as he now is, must drink a slow-working (but painless, Taijé assures me, painless) poison, after which a new king will be chosen to continue the royal work with my wives.

So my life depends upon it. That month, like any other, in spite of my drained condition, I had to prove at least once that *my Pionier of Nature, the sacred Ithyphallian champion, is of all stiff-intruding Blades the primest.* (I see now why these people so readily accepted the words of Maître Rabelais.) And their religion insists that the proof must be shown first at the stake.

Reader, whatever the practices may now be in Paris, I wager that you too would fail if tied naked to a post with raging dysentery and a bag over your head. It was impossible. But my wives so fear that their next master must be Friar John, a tyrant whom they detest, that they amended the ritual a little on my behalf. I was allowed to give the necessary proof alone with Taijé in the small room.

I emerged to the waiting crowd this last month with just one single piece of fruit, of which more later. Meanwhile I wish to set down that my wives, nursing me back to health, found firm proof that I had been poisoned. The culprit, F.J.

[15 July 1561]

If he poisons me again, I shall not be the only one to go. I have explained to them that in Christian countries all great men, kings and lord chamberlains alike, have a taster of their food to guarantee its wholesomeness. Friar John and I now share this safeguard. I have appointed his obsequious friend Pihun to perform this office for me. In the future, if the treacherous Friar adds to my porridge of manioc root any of his secret concoctions (they have many from jungle plants to give venom to their arrows), his main ally in parliament will suffer sooner than me the pangs of flaming entrails.

And yet, so cool is he in his devilry, he might well be willing to carry us both off together (as in chess, sacrificing a foot-soldier for a king). For that reason, my much-valued reader in a future Paris (or Lyons or Geneva or Tours or Valmonay or even tiny Thierry-le-Bois, sometimes the great world outside this jungle valley seems painfully attractive), it is important that I set down exactly how I came to be here. For if my monthly reports are found, and if these savages are then practising a somewhat unusual form of Christianity, you will not otherwise understand how the Book of Maître Rabelais, or one particular part of it, came to be so much revered.

I have told you of my arrival at Fort Coligny after a long and dangerous sea voyage from France. And I have told you about the argument between the three ministers and the Chevalier de Villegagnon on the matter of the Real Presence (or the Unreal Absence) in the consecrated bread. There I take up my story again, when five of us with Sieur de la Taille rowed across the bay to adventure among the savages on the mainland.

[Here Jacques repeats his account of their life in the village of the headman Kuatu – see the entries for 19 January and 17 February 1561, pp. 95–101 – forgetting that he has already included these scenes in his monthly reports. There is not sufficient new detail in this second version for it to be worth including. The narrative resumes after de la Taille has escaped from Villegagnon's soldiers and has vanished into the jungle.]

We could only assume that Sieur de la Taille was dead, having no provisions with him of any kind. After a week of searching, the soldiers drove the five of us roughly along jungle paths, roped together waist to waist. At the coast our own hidden boat awaited us, together with theirs. Still wearing the indignity of chains we were forced, like galley slaves, to row ourselves and our captors to Fort Coligny. The last time we landed there, in the *Grande Roberge*, we had been greeted by a sober-suited Villegagnon and had celebrated our safe arrival with divine worship on the beach, conducted according to correct reformed principles. We could hardly expect another such welcome.

[13 August 1561]

We did not even see the Chevalier. A small ship was anchored off the island and the soldiers made us row directly to it. It had my own name, being called the *Jacques*. On board we found Maître Richier, the only one of our three ministers still at Fort Coligny, accompanied by all our party from Geneva together with three of Villegagnon's men who had come over to our cause. After friendly greetings, and solemn prayers of thanksgiving for our reunion, we learnt that during our absence the governor of the colony had resumed ever more offensively his papistical practices, as a dog will return to its vomit, until Maître Richier decided there was no chance of establishing under such authority any truly Christian settlement. He therefore arranged for this vessel to carry home to France our little Christian community.

Villegagnon, finding about this same time evidence of our habitation on the mainland, had sent soldiers to fetch us, determining that all those who disagreed with him should depart together. On the surface all remained friendly enough, for Maître Richier, being old and wise [fifty-six], played for all our sakes the role of peace-maker. He went on shore each day to arrange provisions for the journey, and on the morning when we were to weigh anchor [4 January 1558] he brought from the Chevalier a message, saying that as he had welcomed our arrival so he regretted our departure, but that he understood the force of true religious conviction, deeply felt, knowing it *from his own experience* [the ironic emphasis must derive from Jacques's manuscript, transcribed by da Caminha], adding that he sympathised with our brave decision and wished us all God speed. This message, as I later discovered, was itself mere diplomacy, designed to brighten a little Villegagnon's black name if we came safely back to Geneva. But it influenced profoundly the course of my own life. Without it I would not now be here.

We were only four days from land, and with a contrary wind had travelled not more than five leagues [approx. 15 miles, 24 km] when news came that the sailors serving their watch on the bilge pumps were working without cease and yet the level was higher in the hold when they ended than when they began. The water had risen above the cargo of red Brazil wood and it belched the colour of blood from the hoses, as if it were a sign from the Lord, staining the sea around us.

After much exertion the hold was made sufficiently dry for inspection. As a joiner, I was invited down with the ship's carpenter and others. I shall never forget that sight. We were afloat in a soft sieve. There were cracks through which the sea spurted in vigorous jets; in many places the wood was spongy to the touch; and where it dried a little, above the water line, there lived a healthy colony of woodworms. I felt like a man inspecting the inside of his coffin.

The carpenter staunched the worst of the cracks with the help of lead, canvas and a plentiful supply of thick grease, so that those on the pumps could once more hold their own. Meanwhile, on deck, a debate was in progress about whether to turn back. The captain of the vessel, a blackguard by the name of Baudouin, argued that if he returned to land his crew would surely desert and he would lose his precious cargo. For him, a man of commerce, the choice was simple: France or death, either was preferable to financial ruin. But he would provide a boat for any who preferred the perils of Villegagnon to the perils of the deep.

Maître Richier trusted to God in the matter of the ship's seaworthiness and urged our party to remain on board. I, on the other hand, had seen for myself the condition of the timbers. I therefore proposed that we return to Fort Coligny, whose governor after all had sent us good wishes on our departure (as I said before, this deceitful message weighed strongly with me). I solicited others to join me, and in the end we were five in the small boat, ready to row away from the *Jacques*. Two came because they had disagreed with Richier about our departure from the island, believing that our reformed mission should continue in Antarctic France. These were Pierre Bourdon and Matthieu Verneuil. One, Jean du Bordel, confessed that he came from a terror of the sea (I would add a passion for manioc beer, easily available in Fort Coligny but in short supply on the *Jacques*). And my friend from Geneva days and earlier, André Lafon, had been easily convinced by my report on the ship's condition.

There had been desperate and prolonged indecision between Oyster John and Nicolas Raviquet, normally inseparable. John was for Fort Coligny, while Nicolas was for France. One moment they would go on together, the next they would return in our boat. We were insisting on immediate departure when Oyster John climbed down among us after tearful farewells, Nicolas Raviquet remaining on board. But at the very last moment, when there was already a bright patch of water between ourselves and the ship, Nicolas cried out in a loud voice, 'My good friend, do not go', whereupon Oyster John changed his mind for the last time and with many helping hands clambered back on board. We passed up his possessions. From them he took the Bible which had belonged to Sieur de la Taille. Knowing that I had none of my own, he threw it down to me, saying that this at least must remain for the Lord's sake in Antarctic France.

In this manner, on the tide of the moment, Oyster John departed to his death. Even if that hulk of worms, my unfortunate namesake, could limp across the fierce ocean back to France, the weight of water in her bilges would slow her so much that her human cargo must die of famine before reaching land.

I treasured, Lord, the Bible that he gave me, until You took it in the torrent. And I pray now for the soul of my good friend Oyster John, lost unnecessarily at sea.

[Jean de Léry lived for another fifty-five years, having been only twenty-four when Jacques last saw him. He died in 1613, in the Swiss canton of Vaud.]

[12 September 1561]

There can be no peace with this Friar John. Last month I returned to the palace, after my two weeks in parliament, to find Taijé in a flaming rage and in no state at all for *foramination*. Her back was covered in such weals that she must sleep face down in her hammock. Any consolation I could give her was limited to unguents prepared for her by my other wives.

She told me this had happened two days before, when I was away hunting with some of the members of parliament. Others had stayed in the village with Friar John to supervise the troglodytes, who are now busy constructing a great stage for the *Representation of the Passion*.

The Friar came into the palace that day – insisting on his right to do so, as he often does between full moon and new moon when I am away from my wives – and he found Taijé, amid much laughter, teaching to my newest wife Beiju and to some of the others certain French words, many of them unknown to Friar John for they come neither in the Book nor within the scope of my lessons in parliament, being private matters.

Taijé was acting out some of the phrases (in gross enough form, she freely admits, for I have found that women among themselves have nothing to learn from men in the enjoyment of lewd entertainment), and it seems that these harmless frolics, worthy of an enchanting Maîtresse Rabelais (for such she is, such she is) were not appreciated by the stern Friar. And it provoked him to an unparalleled fury that she continued to spread a tongue expressly forbidden by him for women and troglodytes. He shoved Taijé and Beiju, knocking them to the ground, yelled at the other girls and stormed out of the palace.

They were astonished at his violence but even more relieved at his departure, so there was laughter and calm again by the time he returned, bringing with him Pihun and three other members of parliament. The Friar carried now a green bamboo, newly cut in the jungle. He swung this at them, and, while my wives scattered in terror, Pihun and one other grabbed Taijé. Holding an arm each, they pulled her against the pillar in the courtyard, her face and belly and breasts against the hard wood (the very stake to which I am tied every month in such playful ceremony), while the Friar struck her with his bamboo, shouting in Tupinili either 'No French' or 'No obscenities', pausing only to speak softly in her ear, 'You hear that?' And so it went on. 'No French. No obscenities. No French. No obscenities. (You understand?) No French. No obscenities. No French. (Can you feel it?) No French. No obscenities. No French', so many times that Taijé now has no idea except just many, many, many, to which her back bears witness still (though I pray by now sufficiently recovered to play her part once more in the *double backed and two bellied Beast*).

The Friar did not come into the palace during the two weeks after I discovered my poor Taijé awaiting me face down in an invalid's hammock in the small room. My first confrontation with him was in parliament after the distribution of the full moon fruit (two pieces only, sorrowfully seeded with two of my older wives, purely as a matter of state and more as a courtesy to them than from any lusty choice of my own). I decided to attack according to the Book, for thus are all important matters now decided in parliament. I concealed my anger, for the moment, in ceremony.

[From now on in the *Monthly Reports* Jacques saves space by giving only the initial letters of the phrases borrowed from Rabelais. They are easily identified and I have expanded them to their original form.]

Jacques le Balleur: *My Harcabuzing Cod and Buttock-stirring Ballock, Friar John* (I omitted *My Friend*, which caused a shout or two of protest from the floor), *I pray thee, favour me so much as to believe* that I have a complaint against thee. It is written of my wives that *lying under thy Wings, thou mayest be Night-Protector of their Sister-hood.* Instead thou art become Day-Persecutor of their Sisterhood. Thou knowest to what deed I refer, committed by thee with Pihun and some others. Now *deal plain with me, and fall down-right square upon the business, without going about the Bush with frivolous circumstances, and unnecessary reservations. Let this serve for the first part of the Sermon.*

Friar John tried to answer, as ever, by the Book. '*It is written so, Billy,*' he protested.

I knew then that I had him, for it is *not* written so. 'Oh, *my Metropolitan Cod*?' said I. 'It does not seem to me that *thou speakest in very deed pertinently, and to purpose.* Where is it written so?'

He was mine, yet he showed still every sign of enjoying himself. He took the bone from his lower lip and stuck his tongue through the hole to moisten it (that vile habit of his when about to launch into a peroration) and then he struck up his quoting stance. But what was there to quote?

Friar John: 'Is it not written *Take thee a Wife, and furbish her Harnish to some tune: Swinge her Skin-coat, as if thou wert beating on Stock-fish*? Which we expound thus: *swinge*, to flog or whip; *Skin-coat*, poetic for skin; *Stock-fish*, a fish so tough that it must be beaten hard before it is fit for cooking, the point of the simile being the necessary hardness of the beating. I took a Wife — yours, Billy — and swinged her as the Book says. *It is written so, and it is holy stuff, I warrant you.*'

I could not believe my ears. Such shameless sophistry over a text which I had so often correctly glossed for them. Now the loathsome creature was carefully replacing the bone, plugging the hole in his lower lip with an exaggerated flourish, as he always does when pleased with himself. He sat down to prolonged applause from his friends on the floor.

In vain did I protest that he had omitted the second half of the passage, which reveals it plainly to be a metaphor for *Venerian thwacking* and not a case of literal *swingeing*.

[The full passage goes: *Take thee a Wife, and furbish her Harnish to some tune: Swinge her Skin-coat, as if thou wert beating on Stock-fish, and let the repercussion of thy Clapper from her resounding Metal, make a Noise, as if a Double Peal of Chiming-Bells were hung at the Cremasters of thy Ballocks.* (lines 20–5)]

The matter hinges on the meaning of *thy Clapper*. I proved to them that in context this means the *Codpiece* or *stiff God of Gardens*. The Friar insisted instead that it meant the instrument of swingeing, in his case the bamboo, the change to Venerian matters coming only with the second *as if*.

'The Book makes plain', he argued, 'that the swingeing must be sufficiently hard to make a Noise *as if a double Peal of Chiming-Bells were hung at the Cremasters of thy Ballocks*. And I do think', he concluded, causing loud laughter from Pihun, 'that those who had the privilege of being present on that occasion will agree that the swingeing was indeed for that purpose sufficiently hard.'

Taijé, Taijé.

[11 October 1561]

All is peaceful now, as everyone prepares for the *Representation of the Passion*.

As a novice I was sent one year to help with the mystery play at Valmonay, during the feast of Corpus

Christi, so I organise now with some authority the making of the houses for the great stage here and the sewing of costumes – a difficult business, this, for people accustomed to going naked, but with the fabric they make for their hammocks, and with colours from ripe jungle fruits, we shall have something suitable at least for Yourself, Lord, both Father and Son, and for Your Blessed Mother. My only sorrow, lacking gunpowder, is that we shall have no fireworks for the ears and arses of the devils.

We are working in parliament on the lines for the chief actors. I am to play the Son, for none of the savages is willing to die, even with the certain promise of resurrection. The Friar has chosen to represent the Father (pleased no doubt that he, and he alone, may create the world, for the play will go back to first things) and Pihun, rightly to my mind, is to be chief devil, whether Satan, Beelzebub or snake.

The chief devil brings me back to the Chevalier de Villegagnon, for while all goes on merrily here I must tell you more of how I came to be a king among savages.

While Oyster John and the others sailed east to certain death, our small party rowed for more than a night and a day, fearful of the wind blowing us ever further from land, until at last we reached the bay and Fort Coligny. We were received coldly. As shipwrecked mariners, the only survivors of a foundered vessel, we could hardly be denied shelter. But we five lived among the papists on sufferance. Their worship was now unashamedly Roman, Masses being conducted by two priests recently arrived from the Sorbonne. We were not expected to attend, our high principles being well known, but neither were we permitted to engage in worship of our own, for we had no minister among us.

So things passed for several months while we bided our time, sharing in the work of the colony but chiefly waiting for a ship that might carry us safely back to France. Late one evening Jean du Bordel, unusually drunk even for him, was arrested on Villegagnon's order and was imprisoned in the fortress. In the morning news reached us that he had been savagely flogged and thrown into an underground cell to subsist for two weeks on nothing but brackish water.

At the time the cause of this affront was given out simply as 'blasphemy', which we took to be an attack on our reformed faith. In fact, Jean himself was partly to blame. We had, secretly among ourselves, a phrase for visiting the jakes. We called it 'going to Mass'. We discovered later that during the night Jean, awash with manioc beer and needing urgently to relieve himself, had told his gaolers that he wished to go to Mass. They, taking this for a sign that he would rejoin their misguided faith, sent to wake one of the Sorbonne priests. He, replying that he would willingly hear the sinner's confession, put on his soutane and hurried to the small building which they used there as a church. Here the guards brought Jean. The priest was awaiting him at the door of the building but all that Jean saw, in his urgent need, was the first upright wall available to him since emerging into the night air. He accordingly did what he had asked permission to do and urinated against it, an arm's length from the outraged priest. The governor was immediately informed and the flogging followed at the fortress without further ceremony.

We woke to hear that our comrade, bleeding and uncared for, was lodged underground and condemned to a long spell of starvation. Pierre Bourdon and Matthieu Verneuil, ever the most holy and fearless in our little party, decided that this act of religious persecution by the papist governor required a corresponding act of religious defiance. As a gesture, and perhaps intemperately, they administered Communion to each other in the open place which served as the town square of the settlement, following the order of service authorised by Maître Calvin even though neither was an ordained minister. In their defence they could point to the priesthood of all believers, but in the eyes of Villegagnon their act was blasphemy indeed, involving the blessed sacrament. A trial of sorts followed, in which my two friends had no part to play other than the glorious role of martyrs. (This was a role which André Lafon and I would eagerly have shared with them had we been in time to join in their act of worship, but we were regrettably delayed on tradesmen's matters in another part of the island.)

After hearing weasel words from the two Sorbonniers, Villegagnon sentenced Bourdon and Verneuil without further ado to death by drowning. For good measure he included in this punishment the unfortunate Jean du Bordel, who had already been whipped to death's door just for a disrespectful phrase and for pissing against the wrong wall.

These three went to their martyrs' deaths from the side of a boat, their hands tied behind their backs and a slab of stone against their bellies. Comfort them now in Your bosom, Lord.

[Jacques here provides an intriguing footnote to recorded history. In Huguenot tradition these three, drowned at Fort Coligny, are listed together as martyrs for the faith. It would seem that the chronicles have taken too much for granted the high idealism of the luckless but aptly named Jean du Bordel.]

André and I, having accidentally been spared the fate of our friends, felt it prudent not to impose further on the hospitality of the papists. At the first opportunity we borrowed a boat and slipped away to the mainland, taking with us the tools of our respective trades. Here, among savages, we knew we could rely on the friendship denied us by so-called Christians.

We found our way with some difficulty back to the village of Kuatu, bringing with us only our personal belongings (mine including still the four volumes of Maître Rabelais, with the addition now of Sieur de la Taille's Bible). We had none of the cheap Honfleur trinkets which had so pleased these people on our previous visit. Our welcome was therefore less warm than before, and our fears for our own safety increased when Kuatu showed us, a few days after our arrival, an engraving of the Virgin Mary. Was he in friendly contact now with our greatest enemies, the Portuguese? He would not say.

We were desperate, André and I, to know where next we might turn for safety, when the Lord sent what seemed little short of a miracle. A boy arrived in the village, very tired after travelling for many days. He had with him a carefully folded leaf, of a kind which I would now recognise more readily than I did then. At its uncreased centre there was French writing in a very black ink. The message was:

To Pierre Richier or any other brother in Christ. Savages here ready for God, hungry for His word. But we have no Bible. Eagerly awaited by all, the Book will ensure conversion. Bring urgently, using this boy as a guide. Antoine de la Taille, Minister.

We needed no urging, André and I. We allowed the boy sufficient time to recover his strength and then set off with him into the jungle – just as de la Taille himself had more than a year before, from this same village, leaving behind him the Bible which, in a notable example of God's merciful pattern, I was now about to deliver to him again.

[10 November 1561]

Our journey began through the thickest jungle I had ever attempted to penetrate. You know the feeling of walking into cobwebs in a dark place? This was a hundred times worse because fleshier. Succulent green tendrils and sticky leaves clutched at every limb as we forced our way slowly through.

After a day of this we came to a river and lay down on its bank, exhausted. The boy knew which fruits of the jungle we could eat, though it was these, I believe, which later brought on the flux. Our route from now on was up the river. Reader, you may imagine perhaps a water journey from Paris to the forest of Fontainebleau? It was not so. We had no boat. Our progress was by edging along the bank in those parts where the river ran deep, or by clambering from rock to rock where it broke into shallow torrents. Hot slow work.

The deep parts were the worst. As we scrambled through the trees overhanging the water, the boy pointed to long floating logs with gnarled bark which drifted in the sun nearby. These, he said, were notorious monsters living in this river. Their hope was to tempt unwary travellers who might approach them (considering them perhaps useful timber for some necessary purpose or, at the very least, mere harmless driftwood), whereupon the log would suddenly open great jaws, with rows of sharp teeth, and would devour the hapless pilgrim. I believe such monsters have never yet been described in Paris. If I had been able to return, I would have published a broadsheet of this same monster, showing him with a French noblewoman clasped tightly in his jaws, her blood dripping from his pointed teeth, and so would have earned for myself a few *sous* in recompense for these pains of travelling.

The boy was very particular that we should never so much as trail a foot in the deep water where this Leviathan lives, for fear of losing it in the monster's gullet. In these difficult circumstances André and I abandoned our tradesmen's tools, which at other times we would always keep by us but which were too heavy to lug to an uncertain destination.

Our baggage now was only books. We were like a pair of chapmen who had lost their way, finding themselves in a most unlikely place for a quick sale. But we could hardly unburden ourselves of books such as these. Sieur de la Taille's Bible was the very cause of our journey (and it would be a rash Christian who, for greater ease, would abandon the Word of the Lord). This precious cargo André carried in a capacious pocket in his coat. My own smaller pocket contained still the four little volumes of Maître Rabelais which I had bought in Troyes and which had been my constant companions in all my adventures.

Sometimes the river became shallow and fast flowing. Here the boy said it was safe to scramble through pools and over rocks, for the basking monster dislikes the hurly burly of a torrent. At such times our difficulty lay in keeping dry the precious books, and from this cause I suffered my first loss. I had stepped into a pool which was deeper than it appeared. I stumbled from the shock, and for a moment was in over my head. André pulled me out, but I was wet through and so was Rabelais. I laid the volumes out on a rock to dry in the sun, together with my clothes, while the three of us sat in the shade, eating jungle fruit. Suddenly there was a rushing sound and from the sky dropped a gigantic bird, some kind of eagle, inexpressibly large and fierce. It must have mistaken the wet white pages of Maître Rabelais for a stranded fish. Without pause for deliberation, it seized Book IV in its great talons and soared away. Thus, at one stroke, was my library much reduced.

Disaster struck us two or three days later, while we were climbing the rocks beside a mighty waterfall. The way was steep and slippery. The boy was leading. I followed him. André came behind. Suddenly there was a cry. I turned, and saw André slithering down the rock towards a sheer drop. He caught hold of a plant, and I started down the path towards him. But the roots of the plant were pulling from the cleft in which they lodged.

With a jerk it came free. André went over the edge. The water far below was foaming white. It turned out of sight before becoming calm again. And so he vanished.

I had known him when we first studied in Geneva together. Since then we had shared every experience – the journey to Honfleur, the crossing in the *Grande Roberge*, the expedition with Sieur de la Taille to the village of Kuatu, our capture by the soldiers, the leaking *Jacques* and our escape, first from that watery death and then from another at the hands of the murderous Ville-gagnon, another brief stay with Kuatu, and now this terrible journey. He was my other half. You took him to Yourself, Lord, with a Bible in his pocket, a sure sign of Your esteem and of his good fortune.

In doing so, You deprived these people here of the Book which they were so eagerly awaiting, keeping from them Your holy word. And You gave them instead the more earthly wisdom, better suited at this stage to their own savage ways, of Maître Rabelais.

[9 December 1561]

The boy and I trudged on together (after I had said many prayers for my friend André Lafon). Night followed day followed night up that terrible river in a seemingly endless journey towards Sieur de la Taille.

The next threat to the dwindling library came from the demands of my feet. My shoes, last repaired many months previously by the cobbler at Fort Coligny, were now through in the left sole. Sharp edges of rock tormented my foot. I tried padding the inside with thick jungle leaves. They were pleasantly cool, but too soft to serve more than a few minutes. It was the boy who suggested Rabelais. To his eye the three remaining volumes from the shop of Monsieur Loys seemed to have been devised for this specific purpose, as pads of best-quality shoe-liner.

With Book IV already lost to the eagle, and the pain in my foot persistent, I took little persuading. Nor was there much difficulty in choosing which volume should go. Book III had become my firm favourite, for in the great debate as to whether Panurge should or should not marry there was all the *culbut and foramination* so lacking in Fort Coligny. This was warmer consolation to a lonely ex-monk than the childhood of Gargantua or the abbey of Theleme. So the opening pages of Book I went first as lining, and very soft and comfortable they were – for a while. But soon they were worn away and had to be replaced by the next chapter. Thus I seemed set to work my way through the great work of Maître Rabelais more rapidly than ever before.

The next demand upon Gargantua and Pantagruel was for an even more base purpose. Our diet of ripe fruit had induced in me a severe flux, running as they say both to and on the jakes. Constant griping means constant wiping and that can become painful (these details are Rabelaisian, but so is life). Somewhere in that same first book, I do not remember where [chapter 13], the young Gargantua researches the best wiping materials. He experiments with fennel, with beet, with parsley, with nettles (I too in the jungle made such errors), with lettuce and spinach, with marjoram, with sage, but like me he comes to despair of the vegetable kingdom, which if long continued will remove, as Gargantua himself expounds it, 'all the skin of the tail'. The young giant finds his perfect answer in the downy neck of a living goose, not only pleasantly soft but warm and well shaped for the purpose.

I had no goose up that jungle river (and if I had, would certainly have cooked her). But paper is also known to serve the purpose. So now, being both ill-shod and ill-shat, I was working my way at double speed through Book I and was soon into Book II. But when Book II was finished, I felt suddenly protective towards my favourite, the third book. For a while I returned to leaves beneath my sole and at my arse, walking sore at both places but at this price preserving my last volume.

My resolve was broken by a final misadventure. The boy was standing at the edge of a still pool in the river, helping me on to the rocks where a stretch of rapids began. Suddenly there was a swirl in the water and he disappeared, nearly pulling me in at the same time. The water became red where he had been. Further down the river there was another sudden turmoil and I caught a glimpse of his leg together with the thrashing tail of Leviathan. The monster had seized him, even in that part of the pool which the boy believed shallow enough and safe. He had been a good boy. I offered up a prayer for him.

Now I was alone. Alone in a world inhabited, it seemed, only by wild beasts of unimaginable ferocity. For my comfort I started on Book III, working forwards

from page 1 for my shoe and backwards from the end
for the other purpose.

The boy had said we were nearly at that part of the
river where we would meet men from his tribe. These
would take us up into the hills, where Sieur de la Taille
now dwelt among them. So I persisted on my own,
with great difficulty, in this journey up the river. But
my weakness was now such, and the flux so continuous,
that after about two days I could go no further. I lay
down beneath a large tree by the water's edge, said my
prayers and awaited death.

I fell asleep, I know not for how long, and woke to
feel hands among my clothing. There were savages
squatting all round me, friendly-seeming, and one –
whom I now know to have been Friar John – spoke as
soon as I opened my eyes.

'Où est le Livre?'

'Il n'y a pas de Livre.'

'Comment?'

It was only when he said 'Comment?', with the
frown and the toss of the head which usually accompany that question in our country, that I realised with a
shock that he had spoken, and I had answered, in
French.

This same savage had now found my pocket, and
inside it the last few surviving pages of my library. He
seized them eagerly, turning them over with something
approaching reverence, and then handed them back to
me, saying that I was to read the Book to him.

I was revived somewhat by this preposterous request
– how Maître Rabelais would laugh, I thought, to hear
of a dying man reading his words to ignorant savages

far up an unexplored river in Antarctic France – and so I began at the top of the first pages.

'*Thumping Cod, Bumping Cod, Tumbling Cod, Be-rumpling Cod . . .*'

'What is Cod?' the savage asked.

He was kneeling beside me where I lay. I pointed to his member, so neatly trussed with its cotton bow. He laughed with delight and turned to his fellows, saying *cararan* (their Tupinili word for it) and raising a clenched fist, strongly suggestive of a *Masculinating Cod*.

'C'est un beau Livre,' he said.

1562

Somehow they got me up the steep mountain path which leads to this hidden valley. I remember little of the journey. My first clear memory is of lying in a hammock here, being well cared for with thick manioc porridge (sovereign against the flux) and sinking again and again into blessed sleep.

I woke every time to find Friar John – or Topi Noi as I knew him then – by my side. He was holding in readiness the pages of Rabelais. As my eyes opened he would thrust them towards me, so that we might continue our reading of the Book. Although his French was easily sufficient for a conversation, much of the Rabelaisian text required explanation and our progress was slow. If I had understood then the reason for his intense interest, I would have slipped in a few useful phrases about Your mercy and the coming Judgement, to become for ever after part of their holy writ. But Friar John has a keen memory. I would have had to repeat the same phrases, word for word in the correct place, at every reading. It would hardly have been possible, Lord.

My first and often repeated question to this young savage was: 'Where is Sieur de la Taille?' At first he brushed it aside, thinking me perhaps too ill to receive the news. But eventually I discovered that the minister had recently died, after living among these people for more than a year. His death, apparently, was from natural causes (later I learnt the truth), and young Topi

Noi seemed greatly to grieve the loss of this good
Christian who had especially befriended him, teaching
him French and clearly intending him for his chief
assistant in the task of converting these people.

Gradually I was able to piece together the details of
what had happened to Sieur de la Taille after his escape
from Villegagnon's soldiers. One of the spies sent out by
the savages had seen him, in a very weak condition, by
the same river where they found me. He was the first
man from our old world that they had encountered.
Being a kindly and a curious people, they did not kill him
(the usual response among ourselves to any unknown
creature) but carried him home to this valley, where a
lucky accident caused him to seem in their eyes a bringer
of good fortune, a living talisman.

Soon after his arrival the savages here were attacked by
another tribe (a rare occurrence, this place being so
difficult of access), but instead of several of their people
being killed or taken prisoner, they drove the invaders
off without the loss of a single man, woman or child.
Instead, one of the enemy tribe was captured. That man
was Ramram Ghi.

This happy event gave Sieur de la Taille a special
position. It also gave him confidence, I have no doubt, in
the ultimate success of his mission, with Topi Noi as his
American deacon.

The next fortunate occurrence, as Topi Noi explained
it to me, was the death of their king. Kingship here is not
hereditary, as it is with us. Instead, a group of the more
influential savages appoint the king's successor. They
must choose a man whose exploits have impressed the
tribe, and on this occasion their thoughts turned natur-

ally to the stranger with a pale skin and a beard (one of their legends tells of just such a hero arriving up the river), whom they had themselves rescued from death and who in return had brought them good fortune. And so – in a process of spreading Your Word, Lord, never predicted in the schools of Geneva – Sieur de la Taille became, before me, a king of savages.

There can only have been one new moon between his inauguration and my arrival in this place, for these people will never allow the moon to dwindle to the paring of a finger nail without a king on the throne to renew its strength. It seems to have been the knowledge that he would be king which determined de la Taille to send the boy in search of a Bible.

My understanding of his death has undergone several revisions. At first Topi Noi suggested that he had died of natural causes. Then, when I first saw the shrivelled head which confronts me now, I assumed that he had been sacrificed as part of the new moon festivities, a fate which I also at that time expected. After discovering the pleasant monthly programme of *culbut and foramination*, I came to believe that Sieur de la Taille, a strict minister of God, had refused to commit the sin of fornication (even for a greater good) and so had been killed in anger. Finally I discovered the whole truth, that any king who will not or cannot send out even one fruit as evidence of *Priapaean Prowess* endangers, according to the religion of the savages, the strength of the moon and the sun and the earth and therefore must ritually die, drinking the slow poison. And so he had, shortly before my arrival.

During the last month of Sieur de la Taille's life, he and Topi Noi had frequently promised the people a future event of great significance – the arrival of the Book. This was why Topi Noi and many others were down by the river searching for me, and why Topi Noi seized upon the ten surviving pages of Rabelais. His prestige with the tribe – and there is none more ambitious than Friar John – depended on the coming of a Book. When it came, just as he and the dead king had predicted, Topi Noi's word became paramount here. And I was his natural candidate for the vacant kingship.

[6 February 1562]

Sieur de la Taille is dead because his Geneva principles would not allow him to *culbut and foraminate* with Saracca and others of my older wives. By contrast I, Jacques le Balleur, just one more fornicating monk, am alive. The fruit sent out so far by Taijé and myself alone would, if planted, stock a good monastery garden.

Between Antoine de la Taille and Jacques le Balleur, which is right? The judgement, Lord, must be Yours. But in my defence I would point to the benefits which will come from our mystery play, the preparations for which go on apace. You, in Your wisdom, included in those few pages of Maître Rabelais two Christian passages among all the dross and titillation (which itself was necessary if the savages were to accept the Rabelaisian ramblings as holy writ). One was the mention of the *Representation of the Passion*. The other was the urgent call to salvation which is at the heart of true religion. *Dost*

*thou not know, and is it not daily told unto thee, that the end of
the World approacheth? The Antichrist is already born.* [lines
31–5]

From this I have been able to introduce Your name
into our play. For if, as I have explained to them, the
Antichrist is against the heavenly King (who in our Book
is Pantagruel), then it must follow that the Antichrist is
also the Antipantagruel and that Christ is another name
for that worthy giant. You are now known among these
people, Lord, in somewhat more seemly fashion as
Christ Pantagruel.

Moreover the references to the birth of Antichrist
(Satan in another guise) and to the end of the world span
between them the whole Bible, from Genesis to Revelation, enabling my play to represent not just the Passion
but the whole of recorded history from Creation to
Salvation.

The opening scene serves to demonstrate how greatly
the education of the savages will be advanced. They have
been very ignorant, Lord, about how You created
mankind. They have a foolish and disgusting story
which tells that You first made human beings, to people
the earth, by shooting Your seed into earthenware jars.
These jars, they say, You then covered, ordering that no
one should look inside. After some time a scratching
noise was heard within the jars. You opened them, and
inside were fully formed children.

A five-year-old in France would find it hard to believe
such nonsense, but the story gets worse. A disobedient
woman opened one of the jars to discover what it
contained. A few days later a loathsome smell came from
that jar, and You discovered inside a dead child. In Your

fury You picked it up and threw it into the woman's belly, saying that as a punishment she and all other women must carry children and suffer the pain of giving birth.

Because they never, until now, heard the truth, the people here believed this foolish tale. I have carefully explained to them its errors – how the disgusting idea of Your using in this fashion an earthenware pot is an invention based upon our corrupt human experience of generation, whereas Your actual methods, fashioning Adam from clay and Eve from his rib, were godly in their grandeur and simplicity.

There is a moral here. These people had heard that the Fall came about through the disobedience of a woman (though ignorant that her name was Eve) and they knew of Your fitting punishment for all womankind in the pains of childbirth. Did they therefore once know the whole truth, later forgetting some parts and replacing them with inventions of their own? It must indeed be that a traveller long ago brought them the news of their first parents, as I do now, but that his words were largely forgotten through lack of any ability to write them down. Herein we may see the importance in all true religion of a Book.

Earthenware jars and putrid infants – so many errors, so much foolishness. But all will be amended. My opening scene, as performed also at Valmonay, shows the creation of Adam and Eve by Yourself (called here God Gargantua, since You must be the Father of Christ Pantagruel). There follows the temptation of Eve by the serpent of Antichrist, the eating of the apple and the sewing of aprons. They perform all this with great enthusiasm in rehearsals (Friar John, as God Gargantua, being the most eager of all). Thus, gradually, will decency and right thinking spread among them.

Is not all this a worthy result, Lord, even at the price of a certain amount of *culbut and foramination*, which may endanger my soul (You must indeed be the Judge) but none other?

While on that matter, and on the theme of creation by these more familiar means, I have kept once again to the last my personal good news. Taijé is with child again.

[8 March 1562]

It may not look the way it does at Valmonay, but it will be a pageant to remember.

These savage people have no aptitude for costumes, preferring the fashion of Adam and Eve before the Fall, but they have long been in the habit of making great masks to wear at their own ceremonies. My mask as king in the new moon festivities is but one among many such creations. At any feast there are dancers wearing on their heads and shoulders wicker frames, covered in bark, on which are painted great faces, usually white, often with huge red eyes, a black circle for a mouth and something very like a carrot for a nose. From these masks long grasses hang, from the shoulders almost to the ground, so that nothing is seen below but the feet of the dancers. Such are to be our costumes for the *Representation of the Passion*, and I believe they will serve very well, especially for the *Devils and Devilesses*.

The play is to begin with Friar John, as God Gargantua, creating the human race. He will fashion a lump of moist earth into the shape of a man, whereupon a young naked savage will appear miraculously from behind a screen. This Adam is then to lie on the stage, while Friar John pretends to take his rib, and then Eve in her turn steps from behind the screen. She too of course is naked, as history tells. Then comes Friar John's friend Pihun, with a serpent's mask above his robe of grasses, bearing a jungle fruit, the nearest we can find to an apple, with which he must tempt Eve and she Adam.

All this You will notice, Lord, is the unadorned truth. There is nothing here of the filthy business, in which these savages have until now placed their faith, of ejaculation in earthenware jars. But I have been less successful in the matter of the Flood.

The savages have received from their distant forefathers some report of the Deluge, but for the lack of a written Book it has become garbled in the telling. They know that You sent the waters to cover the earth because of Your displeasure with mankind, but they have heard nothing of Noah or of his ark. Instead they believe that an ancestor of theirs, together with his wife, climbed a tall tree to escape the waters. What about the animals, I ask them? Did the elephant and the camel climb this same tree? They have no answer, but seem unable to understand that such animals would not be alive today if Noah had not built, to Your specification, his ark of gopher wood and taken them in two by two. (Truth to tell, they had not previously heard of either elephant or camel and seem somewhat indifferent to their fate.) It may well be that all the animals in the jungle can climb trees. Thus does error most frequently persist, conforming to partial observation of the truth.

The savages, Lord, are very attached to their version of the Flood and I have failed to interest them in the ark. I regret to tell You that in our play Noah and his bed-fellow will scramble up a tree. Nor have these people heard about the dove. According to them, when Noah wanted to test whether the waters had abated, he had recourse to no more subtle method than throwing down from his perch large nuts, much like coconuts. He judged by the difference between a plop and a thud as to whether it was time yet to descend and set about repopulating the world.

It is impossible to speak from inside these masks of wicker and bark, and this has provided Friar John with another role. He plays now *the Prompter*, as mentioned in Maître Rabelais, in addition to God Gargantua. But unlike our prompter at home, who merely keeps the book and instructs the players when to enter or to speak, Friar John has taken upon himself the burden of telling the story. We, the actors, are to be mute, miming our humble roles while Friar John, wearing something akin to a knight's helmet with visor up, both creates the universe as God and tells its subsequent story as Prompter. As a result he has been of late very much less trouble than usual.

Try as I may, I cannot get them to understand the Annunciation and the Incarnation. We had at Valmonay a dove, propelled by a firework in its tail, which ran on a

wire above the heads of the crowd and exploded in the
side of a great statue of the Virgin, and I had hoped for
something similar if less elaborate here. But they are
perplexed as to Who this dove is (I should have harped
less on Noah's bird), nor can they understand what He
must do to the Virgin, played by my youngest wife,
Beiju. They understand only that the Virgin must
become pregnant and that God Gargantua is to be the
Father of the Child, but they persist in seeing this sacred
Conception in earthly terms. As Friar John approaches
Beiju, he makes a gesture previously unknown to me
which causes laughter and which I fear may suggest to
the minds of these savages *culbut and foramination*. We
shall clarify the finer points on later occasions, Lord.
This is only a beginning.

The most moving moment in the entire play comes
now. Beiju vanishes behind a screen at the same moment
as Taijé appears, visibly pregnant, only to vanish in her
turn and to reappear, a moment later, with a shawl
concealing her shape and with our beloved Rachel in her
arms. This is a scene which will greatly please the
audience.

Soon I make my appearance as Christ Pantagruel,
wearing a mask and grass robes as the others do. I heal
many sick people, I cause the lame to walk, I even give
life to the dead, and I miraculously distribute food to the
audience, while all the time being pestered by many
Devils and Devilesses who, attempting to prevent my
miracles, sally forth from a great Hell mouth which the
Troglodytick People have built and painted to resemble a
dragon's head with open flaming jaws.

This Hell mouth will provide the climax to our play,

for after I am crucified (tied to the cross, not nailed, for fear of accident or over-enthusiasm) and am raised again from the dead, I go to the Hell mouth to conquer the *Devils and Devilesses* and to release from torment all the spirits of the ancestors of the savages. As the dead emerge in jubilation from Hell, I shall myself *enter within the Pit of the Theater.* At that moment all the spectators will themselves run round to the back of the stage and will come through the mouth of Hell to begin the great finale, as promised in the Book, when *on a sudden both Players and Spectators* will *fall into such an exorbitant Temptation of Lust* that there will not be *Angel, Man, Devil, or Deviless, upon the place* who will not then *Bricollitch it with all their Heart and Soul.*

I know that it ends differently at Valmonay, but this general *culbut and foramination* is promised them in their Book. Without that promise we would have no play, and without the play no chance of educating these ignorant people. As You Yourself have said, Lord, we must make the most of our talents.

[6 April 1562]

For the record I have a new wife. Time flies indeed. The chestnut festivities came round again. Her name is Terepik. A very pretty child, but I have been so listless since I was poisoned that I could hardly bring myself to do my duty. But Taijé insisted, and the girl is satisfied.

The real news this month is further hostilities between

Taijé and Friar John. It happened when we were rehearsing the Incarnation. Friar John, as *Prompter*, is very pleased with the business where slim Beiju is instantly transformed, after the attentions of the Holy Spirit, into round-bellied Taijé. During a run-through he turned to Pihun and others, as Taijé appeared from behind the screen, and said, indicating with an obscene gesture his own masculinity, 'Rather quicker work than some I could mention.' It was a joke, albeit a poor one, but Taijé flew at him and knocked him off the platform, and his precious helmet took more than a day to repair. She put her hands on her hips and laughed to see him gather up the pieces of his headgear and scramble up on to the platform to get at her (I had to come between them), and she has considered this a fine revenge for the beating he gave her.

If I were not able to protect her, Friar John would certainly do Taijé much harm, and this has long been the subject of our discussions in the palace. My wives believe that he will try again to do away with me so that he may become king. Then he would play the tyrant legitimately among them, beating them at his slightest whim to enforce obedience. There can be no doubt that he would be my successor on the throne (though he professes that he would never accept this high honour), for Pihun and the others would make him their choice.

I have been trying to prove from the Book that Friar John must not take the place of Panurge, but if anything it suggests the opposite. *By Saint Rigomer (quoth Fryar John) I do advise thee to nothing, (my dear Friend Panurge) which I would not do my self, were I in thy place.*

'Were I in thy place': the very mention of the possibility increases the probability. It will not be safe to go by the Book.

For my wives' comfort there is only one answer. The throne must remain occupied so that the question of inheritance does not arise. To this end I must avoid poison and must retain my vigour *in the practising of my Placket-Racket within the Aphrodisian Tennis-Court at all times fitting.* But here also is a problem, caused I believe by Friar John's attempt to poison me.

In recent months there have sometimes been but two or three pieces of fruit in the dish. Never more than five. The happy times of seventeen (even twenty-six once, the legend goes) seem like some fable of a golden age. The infamous Pihun had the effrontery to raise the matter in parliament. He asked whether he might bring a passage from the Book to the attention of the house, and in particular to the attention of His Majesty. Then he quoted the whole section from the wet nurses to the doctors of law (and they all joined in, for they enjoy nothing so much as a full-throated recital of holy writ), while I, assuming for the occasion an air of the gravest indifference, must sit like a schoolboy being rebuked for insufficient effort.

[*If there pass long intervals betwixt the Priapising Feats, and that thou make an intermission of too large a time, that will befall thee, which betides the Nurses, if they desist from giving suck to children, they lose their Milk; and if continually thou do not hold thy Aspersory Tool in exercise, and keep thy Mentul going, thy Lactinician Nectar will be gone, and it will serve thee only as a Pipe to piss out at, and thy Cods for a Wallet of lesser value than a Beggars Scrip. This is a certain truth I tell*

thee, Friend, and doubt not of it; for my self have seen the sad
experiment thereof in many, who cannot now do what
they would, because before they did not what they might have
done. Ex desuetudine ammittuntur Privilegia. *Non-usage*
oftentimes destroys ones Right, say the learned Doctors of the
Law. (lines 70–84)]

My answer was simple and dignified. 'By *long inter-*
vals is signified one full moon to the next. Has the dish
ever lacked fruit? Has the crescent moon paused in its
growth? Quote me no quotations until they are needed.'

'Until they are needed . . . '

It was just a phrase. We often use such phrases. 'As
long as I live', 'Till death us do part', 'God willing'. We
say them unthinkingly, without constantly renewed
speculation as to how long may indeed remain to us.
And the reason for that easy indifference is that You
alone know our allotted span. It extends or shrinks
through no will of ours. We cannot bid our heart to
beat, nor shall our fears cause it to cease, whatever
rumour may say. But I, most pitiable of men, am in a different position. Monthly I must prove my right to live.
Whores fornicate for a living. I fornicate for life itself.

At present these gloomy fears are far from everyone's
mind, for we are in the high season of *culbut and forami-*
nation. This last new moon was the chestnut festival,
when all the savages indulge themselves, and the next is
the time arranged for the *Representation of the Passion*.
The play will be performed on the last day of the old
moon, and when I have led all the people through the
mouth of Hell, delivering them over to the promised
exorbitant Temptation of Lust, I shall myself retire into the
palace, to be alone with Taijé and the others.

This coming month, surely, after the excitement of the play, there will be a plentiful harvest of fruit.

[6 May 1562]

A few moments ago I discovered something so startling that I know not yet how to describe it. I shall tell you all that happened, from the beginning.

The play started about midday, but the audience had by then spent several hours in preparing themselves. Not a single person in the tribe would miss this *Representation of the Passion* and each must be decked out in finery suitable for the occasion. From dawn they were daubing each other with pigments, men and women alike. They begin usually with a small dot in the centre of the cheek, from which they make a line outwards, in a spiral, changing the colour from time to time, until each side of the face is filled and the two patterns intertwine on the forehead. Similar decoration is provided for arms, bellies and legs. The designs are so drawn that the effect is of elegance rather than savagery.

Even in this remote valley some of the women have necklaces of the glass beads brought to Brazil by the French and the Portuguese, but those who lack such riches have found a simple alternative. The skills required to paint patterns on the skin can provide also a very passable necklace of beads, and a necklace more-over which will conveniently lie flat when it comes to dancing and which cannot be mislaid during *culbut and foramination*. Some of the women also wear a special necklace for such occasions, of their own savage devising, which is made from a dried root called *piripiriwa*. This root gives off a powerful smell and is said to be a great stimulant to *Priapising Feats*.

Soon after midday the entire tribe was packed into the central square, between palace and parliament, in a state of high expectation. The stage ran across the open end of the square, with the jungle as a backcloth, and a roar went up when Friar John stepped forth (from a house built on the stage to represent heaven) to begin the business of creation. There were shouts of approval when he made Adam from clay, and a deep interest, deriving from a genuine thirst for knowledge among these people, when he seemed to remove one of Adam's ribs, holding up in triumph a bloody bone (hidden nearby in the floor of the stage) from which he fashioned Eve.

The story of the Flood was more boisterous than we had intended, for when Noah and his wife were safely up their tree and wished to test the level of the waters by their device of coconuts, instead of dropping the said coconuts on to the stage they used them for pelting the audience. This caused no resentment but a great deal of good-natured laughter, as spectators hurled the nuts back at the stranded patriarch, falling short of his tree and clattering against the houses on the stage. Here was unexpected proof to Noah that the waters had subsided, even if they seemed on this occasion not to have swept away all humankind but himself and his wife. (There was no room in the tree, nor in the savages' own account of the story, for Ham, Shem and Japheth with their brides. I did not insist upon them, but I admit that our version of the Flood remains, at present, somewhat deficient in historical fact.)

I mention these details because it is important to know, if the conclusion of all this is to be understood, how much excitement there was in this crowd of savages as they watched the performance. It was excitement with a specific end in view, for during the weeks and months of rehearsal our play had become well known. Every member of that audience was aware of what was to happen after I, Christ Pantagruel, had led the spirits of the ancestors up from the darkness of Hell into the light of day. And it was for that moment, as much as for the play itself, that all the painting had been lovingly carried out and the necklaces chosen. Actors and audience together seemed to hurry us through scene after scene towards our climax.

That is not to say that the underlying message of the play (its justification, Lord) did not reach these people with the force of revelation. What cheers there were when I performed my miracles of healing and feeding. Cheers too when I was crucified (I am not sure why, in this case), cheers again when I rose from the grave, and cheers when I overwhelmed Pihun, the Devil, and beat and chained him. The greatest cheers of all were when I broke down the gates of Hell to release the worthy spirits. The excitement of some of the men in the audience was by then plain to see (a powerful argument for getting these savages at some future date into breeches), as they rushed with their women to form the queue which would pass through the mouth of Hell and then disperse into the jungle around, for the purpose specified in the Book of Maître Rabelais.

Friar John, as stipulated, was the first to vanish [*The Prompter forsook his Copy*] and he was soon followed off the stage by Pihun [*yea, Lucifer got out of his Fetters*]. I myself wandered for a while in the square, as is required [*entered within the Pit of the Theater*] and went also into the jungle behind the stage, for I needed to witness sufficient of the *Bricollitching* to justify my own withdrawal. [*Seeing the huge Disorder, I disparked my self forth of that inclosed place, in imitation of Cato the Censor, who perceiving by reason of his presence, the Floralian Festivals out of order, withdrew himself.* (lines 186–9)]

And so it was that I came upon the scene from which my mind recoils still. Behind the stage was Friar John, in the act. Nothing strange in this, for everyone else was at it; and though he has not previously shown any sign of human affection, he must be a man like other men.

Not in this respect, Lord. Beneath him, face down in the moist jungle soil, was Pihun. *Friar John, my Friend; Buttockstirring Ballock* indeed.

I shall be surprised if the villain visits the palace this next two weeks, but after that I shall shame him for this indecency. Meanwhile, with the cries of 'Suruk suruk' sounding vigorously from the jungle outside, and with this very disturbing monthly report now complete, I must repair to my own private festivities.

[4 June 1562]

My wives will become impatient. Instead of writing I have stared and stared this morning at the shrivelled head of Sieur de la Taille. It seems to grin at me, in a manner quite unlike his severity in life, as if delighting in the secret which he holds from me. Is he the victim of calumny? Or am I betrayed in him?

I decided not to raise my complaint against Friar John in parliament, but expressed my outrage to him privately. He feigned surprise at my indignation, admitting without apparent shame that women held no appeal for him, being creatures, as the Book says, *unsatiable and gluttonous in their Voluptuousness*. Without giving me a chance to interrupt, or even to suggest the full force of my disapproval, he was off on his favourite subterfuge, that of quotation.

'*I am not ignorant*' – he emphasised this point with an airy gesture of the arm – '*that Salomon said, who indeed of that matter speaketh Clerk-like, and learnedly: as also how Aristotle after him declared for a truth, That for the greater part, the Lechery of a Woman is ravenous and unsatisfiable* (lines 134–7). Indeed, *Billy*, I am myself of their opinion and must in all honesty declare that *if Womens things cannot be satiated*, then for *such a gill* I have no *fit Jack*.'

I told him not to call me Billy when there was serious contention between us. And I retorted, with considerable heat, that if for *such a gill* he had no *fit Jack*, when it came to *Buttockstirring* elsewhere he seemed fit enough.

'Ah,' he said, 'but therein lies the difference. For Lucifer you will find (should you make the experiment) is far from *unsatisfiable*.'

I asked him – foolishly, without sufficient fore-thought – whether he did not remember the fate of Sodom. He did not (that being in the other Book), but he begged me to tell him what happened.

So I explained how two angels of the Lord came to stay with Lot in Sodom, and how the sight of such male beauty excited beyond all endurance the wicked Sodom-ites who came crowding round Lot's house, demanding that the strangers be released unto them for the easing of their unnatural desires, and how Lot pleaded with them, saying that he could not fail thus in the duties of hospitality. Instead Lot offered, for the allaying of the aroused passions of the crowd, to send out to them his two virgin daughters, innocent as yet of the attentions of any man, that the lusty fellows might indulge them-selves with these maidens in whatever manner they wished, so long as they did not trouble his guests. [Jacques embroiders a little, but his basic narrative follows Genesis 19: 4–11.] The Sodomites rejected Lot's daughters and pressed so hard to come at the angels that they nearly broke down the door. Then the angels stirred themselves to protect Lot and they smote the crowd with blindness, the very punishment visited also upon Onan. [It is clearly a long-lasting popular fallacy, this linking of blindness with the sin of Onan – in its modern meaning as opposed to the *coitus interruptus* which is Onan's offence in the Bible. In fact the Lord was not concerned with Onan's eyesight and simply slew him, Genesis 38: 10.]

'Onan?' asked Friar John, much interested. 'Who is Onan?'

'That is another story. Let us keep to the heresy in

question. Pantagruel was so incensed against the people of Sodom that he destroyed their city, with fire and brimstone, for the very crime which you and your little friend Pihun were openly committing after the *Representation of the Passion*. Destroyed their native city. With fire and brimstone.'

Friar John removed the bone from his lower lip and ran his tongue round, in that offensive manner of his, to moisten the edges of the cavity.

'Did Papai Hu know this?' he asked. Papai Hu is his name for Sieur de la Taille. 'Did he know this story about Sodom?'

'Of course.'

'Well, it didn't stop *him*.' He smiled at me. The disgusting man-child (he is small for his age) smiled at me as he said these words.

'What do you mean by that?' I understood perfectly well what he meant (in a flash that came like a blow somewhere deep in the bowels), but it came out instinctively, this question that one asks, knowing and dreading the answer, when there seems nothing else to say. 'What *do* you mean by that?'

'It was Papai Hu who showed me,' said the Friar, as calmly as if we were discussing the furnishing of parliament. 'My instruction was under him, you might say, just as Pihun's has been under me. It was because of our friendship that he taught me French and I arranged for him to be king. But I did not understand, then, that *carapua* was as disgusting to him as it is to me. And he did not understand the duties of kingship among our people. That was our mistake. And my great loss.'

He looked straight at me as he said this, daring to

suggest that his grief for Sieur de la Taille was a noble sentiment after the filth he had implied. I was too disturbed to reply, ending the interview abruptly and without the moral authority I had intended. And I am still too disturbed, confronted now by the mortal remains of Papai Hu, to know what I must believe.

My wives used to laugh, with some embarrassment, when I asked about his death. I understood their embarrassment when I learnt that a failure of *Priapaean Prowess* must lead, for a king, to death by slow poison. Sieur de la Taille had not *practised his Placket-Racket* within my wives' *Aphrodisian Tennis-Court*. But did he die for refusing to practise it, as I had assumed? Or from inability to practise it, seeing no charm in Lot's daughters?

My wives will not be able to tell me, since to them the two would seem alike, having the same result. I stare one final time into his tight-drawn eyes and flared nostrils. No hint there. On this matter I must remain for ever in tormented ignorance.

[4 July 1562]

I have never known such a loss. I grieved when my good friend André Lafon was swept away in the river. I was heartbroken after I had walked eight days from the monastery on the news of my mother's illness and arrived to find that she had given up the ghost just one hour previously, asking after me, her only son. But these were nothing to the emptiness of the world today. The sun shines as before, there must still be flashes of bright feathers in the jungle, women's hands do their best to soothe, children clasp my knees or pull my beard as if nothing has happened, but the spirit has gone from all these pleasant things now that Taijé is dead.

My single happiness is to sit imagining her as she was, thereby increasing my sorrow. Her laughter, her movement, the curves of her body, the glancing provocation of her eyes. That such things should have been. And that they should not be.

I thought at first I would hate the child who killed her. Yet I love him, above all my other children, because Taijé saw him and loved him. Our son. We called him Isaac. She liked the sound of the name and would constantly call for him, when we believed that she was only weak but she knew perhaps that she was dying.

Two chestnut times ago she came to me. A little more than two years. A short time for such a large legacy – this great weight of happiness and sorrow, and two children. Rachel and Isaac. I am content with Isaac. *He will perhaps therewith beget a Male, and so depart the more contentedly out of this Life, that he shall have left behind him one for one.* Rachel for Taijé, one for one also. Through these two she lives, we live together.

My dear reader in Paris, or anywhere else, in some far distant century, sometime or never, have you been lucky enough to love and be loved? I will not breed contention between us. Let us not say prettier, more seductive, more tender, wiser, calmer, more wicked, funnier, more impossible, or in any way either exceeding the other in sweet lascivious charms, but let me only propose that your paragon is equal in all these qualities to mine and beg you to allow the same. I can never describe her. But by this devious route, bringing to mind your own happiness, past or present, perhaps I may lead you into imagining the joyful presence and the grievous loss of one whose very name it seems a sacred and a desperate act to write, large letter by letter,

TAIJÉ

[2 August 1562]

We have had such events as in legend presage the fall of kings. A comet blazed through the sky and was seen for several nights, trailing a feathery tail. [This comet was widely reported during July 1562, and has made possible the precise dating of this monthly report to the subsequent new moon, and thus the dating of all previous ones back to Jacques's arrival in the valley.] And during the days of the comet we were attacked by the tribe of Ramram Ghi.

It is rare for enemies to penetrate this valley, and the disaster has been seen as another ill omen. The attacking savages rescued Ramram Ghi, carrying him off with his child, and they took also three of our young men. Since Ramram Ghi was unharmed here (indeed plump and pampered, though to an unworthy end), it may be that they will not immediately eat these people of ours. But there is talk already of revenge and of an expedition against this enemy tribe, that being the traditional pastime of the savages in Brazil which I had hoped to replace with regular *Representations of the Passion.*

There is talk too of a change of king. Very little fruit has been found in the dish this past month or two, you will understand why. Friar John's plan is not to succeed me himself. I realise now that my wives were wrong to fear this in him, knowing as I do that he would be dead within the month. Instead he intends to place upon the throne some obedient *Codpiece* from parliament, keeping all the power for himself as first minister.

I am no longer of use to him and he attacks me savagely, linking the scarcity of fruit with the comet and other disasters. I in my turn try to persuade the parliament that he, Friar John and no other, must have the honour of succeeding me as king.

Friar John: *By the Blood of a Hog's-pudding, Billy, till when wouldst thou delay the acting of a Husband's part? Dost thou not know, and is it not daily told unto thee, that the end of the World approacheth? By Saint Rigomer, I do advise thee to nothing, (my dear Friend Panurge) which I would not do myself, were I in thy place: only have a special care, and take good heed thou soulder well together the Joynts of the double backed and two bellied Beast, and fortifie thy Nerves so strongly, that there be no discontinuance in the Knocks of the Venerian thwacking, else thou art lost, poor Soul.*

I defended myself against this scurrilous attack with the utmost vigour, weary though I have felt since Taijé's death. The existence of a Book does make argument easier than it might otherwise be:

Jacques le Balleur: *Do not here produce ancient Examples of the Paragons of Paillardise, and offer to match with my Testiculatory Ability, the Priapaean Prowess of the fabulous Fornicators, Hercules, Caesar, and Mahomet, who in his Alchoran doth vaunt, that in his Cods he had the vigour of Threescore Bully Ruffians: but let no zealous Christian trust the Rogue, the filthy ribald Rascal is a Lyar. Shall thou need to urge Authorities, or bring forth the Instance of the Indian Prince, of whom Theophrastus, Plinius, and Athenaeus testifie, that with the help of a certain Herb, he was able, and had given frequent Experiments thereof, to toss his sinewy Piece of Generation, in the Act of carnal Concupiscence, above Threescore and ten times in the space of Four and twenty hours. Of that I believe nothing, the number is supposititious, and too prodigally foisted in: Give no Faith unto it, I beseech thee, but prithee trust me in this, and thy credulity therein shall not be wronged; for it is true, and* Probatum est, *that my Pionier of Nature, the sacred Ithyphallian champion, is of all stiff-intruding Blades the primest.*

Friar John: *Though for the present thou possibly be not weary of the Exercise, yet is it like, I will hear thee confess a few years hence, that thy Cods hang dangling downwards for want of a better Truss.*

Jacques le Balleur: *Thou twittest me with my Grey Hairs, yet considerest not how I am of the nature of Leeks, which with a white Head carry a green, fresh, streight, and vigorous Tail. The truth is nevertheless, (why should I deny it) that I now and then discern in my self some indicative Signs of Old Age.*

(Here I was in subtle manner bringing the topic round to my successor.)

Friar John: *I understand thee well enough. Time makes all things plain. The most durable Marbre or Porphyr is subject to Old Age and Decay.*

Jacques le Balleur: *That is not, the Devil hale it, the thing that I fear; nor is there where my Shoo pinches. The thing that I have the greatest reason to dread is that my wives shall make me a Cuckold.* This, I fear, *is the Lot to which from Heaven I am predestinated.*

Friar John: *If so be it was preordinated for thee, wouldst thou be so impious as not to acquiesce in thy Destiny? Speak thou Jaded Cod, Faded Cod, Mouldy Cod, Musty Cod.*

Jacques le Balleur: *Nay truly, Fryar John, my left Ballock, I will believe thee, for thou dealest plain with me, and fallest down-right square upon the business, without going about the Bush with frivolous circumstances, and unnecessary reservations.* My concern is only, who shall *Bricollitch it* with my wives when I am gone? And – I put it now to the assembled parliament – who better to deputise for me in the *Delights of Venery* than my acknowledged deputy in all things? Friar John is appointed already *my left Ballock* and *Night-Protector* of the *Sister-hood* of my wives. Advising me to allow no *discontinuance in the Knocks of the Venerian thwacking*, he says that he advises me *to nothing which he would not do in my place.* I may indeed *be saved, and have a place in Paradise,* knowing, when I am *weary of the Exercise,* that you, Friar John, *my Ballockette,* shall *practise your Placket-Racket* in my stead *within the Aphrodisian Tennis-Court. Therefore the Heavens be pleased to grant to thee, at all She-conflicts, a stiff-standing Fortune.*

With this fine peroration I proposed that we should

formally adopt Friar John as the man who must in due course *make me a Cuckold*. He put up a vigorous opposition, for reasons well known to himself and to me but which the majority considered a fitting sign of modesty. Being his minions, they were inclined to vote for my resolution and to acclaim him my heir. But being his minions, they were also reluctant to go against his apparent wishes.

He carried the day by arguing that there is no clear evidence in the Book as to whether Friar John shall succeed Panurge. He also quoted the line *Every one (answered Friar John) that would be a Cuckold, is not one*, adding that these are mysterious matters, being *Monachal Topics and Maxims of the Cloyster*. He advised therefore that any decision be postponed – meaning that while I am away in the palace he will influence the members to appoint someone other than himself in my place.

It will indeed be hard to prove from the Book that he must be king. But only thus, it seems, can I protect my wives from his vicious tyranny when I am gone.

[1 September 1562]

Lord, You have decided the matter. By this one small miracle You have made Your wishes plain. I come to You now in the hope that I may indeed *be saved and have a place in Paradise*. As to the fate of Friar John, my mind is at ease. Your will be done.

You are no doubt bemused by this, my sometime-somewhere reader, to whom I now bid farewell. I must tell you with pride that the merciful Lord chose as the instrument of His divine will my beloved Rachel, the first-born of Taijé. She was playing with my old pair of shoes, a favourite toy in the palace ever since I long ago gave up wearing them and went barefoot like my loyal subjects. Her little arm was deep in one of these shoes, which she was attempting to hurl at me. When she set it down, we saw between her fingers a small scrap of paper. Through this fragment the Lord has settled matters here to the lasting benefit of my wives and family.

Have I told you that many of the leaves of Maître Rabelais, so beautifully printed at Troyes, went to plug holes in my shoe leather? After my arrival in this kingdom I soon became weary of elucidating to Friar John and the others those ten pages of Rabelais which had reached them intact, and one day I thought how the many leaves padding my left shoe would cause untold excitement if their origin were discovered. I did not relish the prospect of deciphering a hundred or more pages of text, trodden into a solid brown cake round the edges with the centre of each worn completely away. A lifelong task for a scholar even in the Sorbonne! So I burnt those Rabelaisian remnants and thought no more of them until my darling Rachel, with divine guidance, found the last surviving fragment in the toe. The printed words, as the Lord intended, answered the case *in very deed pertinently*.

When we next met in parliament, after the full moon, Friar John opened by proposing that since there was no clear evidence in the Book as to who should make

Panurge a cuckold and be his successor, the appointment should be left vacant until the unthinkable should occur, with the discovery one month of no fruit at all in the basket (whereupon he, in my enforced absence, would be free to appoint whomsoever he might please). It was plain that they had all agreed together on this policy. 'No clear evidence', nods of agreement. 'Decision should be postponed', wise looks to greet wise counsel.

You may imagine the excitement when I produced the scrap of paper which, even to illiterate eyes, proclaimed itself by the appearance of the text as coming from the Book. One side of the precious fragment was black with dirt, to the point of illegibility. The other was surprisingly clean, having been pressed securely against the upper leather.

They passed the holy relic round among themselves with the deepest reverence, holding it as tenderly as if it were endowed with some fragile life of its own. Meanwhile I described to them, in terms of wonder and mystery, how a little child, unknowing, innocent, at play, had been the instrument of this great discovery *there where my Shoo pinches.*

Jacques le Balleur: And now, will you hear what it says? Will you discover what holy text has been added by this miracle to the Book? Shall I read it?
Parliament: Read it! Read it!
Jacques le Balleur, reading from the scrap of paper: *A Cuckold you will be, beaten and robbed. Then cryed out Friar John with a loud Voice: He tells the truth; upon my Conscience, thou wilt be a Cuckold, an honest one, I warrant thee; O the brave Horns that will be born by thee!*

164

Ha, ha, ha. Our good Master De Cornibus, God save thee,
and shield thee.

[Book III, chapter 14. In the Troyes edition this
passage is 29 leaves before the section which Jacques had
in his pocket when he was discovered.]

When I finished reading, there was an astonished
silence that the message came *in very deed* so *pertinently*
and to purpose. I saw that Friar John was about to raise
objections, so I quickly concluded the matter.

Jacques le Balleur: You will see, my friends, how in this
 text Friar John, with characteristic modesty, apolo-
 gises for what should be a source of pride in him and a
 cause of gratitude in us. While accepting the facts of
 the case (we read how he cried out with a loud voice,
 He tells the truth), he admits openly that it is he, Friar
 John, who is to be the instrument of cuckoldry, taking
 upon his conscience the responsibility for the act (*upon*
 my Conscience, thou wilt be a Cuckold). It remains only
 to me to greet *my Harcabuzing Cod and Buttockstirring*
 Ballock, Friar John, my Metropolitan Cod, and to proclaim him *my left Ballock*, indeed my own *Ballockette*,
 and, in plain language, my worthy and *preordinated*
 successor.

There was such clamour of congratulation as they
crowded round to hail their prince that the unfortunate
Friar had no further chance to avoid his fate. He follows
me where I now go, and but one month later.

Lord, You know me for what I am and have been. A
fornicating monk (though in this but one among many);

a reformed Christian, for the most part faithful to the high standards of Geneva; and latterly a king, committed in the interests of the state to a regular programme of *culbut and foramination*. You and You alone shall be my Judge. I crave Your mercy. You submit me now to a final test, requiring me to resist the seductive charms of my wives, whose contrary duty it is to arouse and satisfy me. This time, with Your help, I shall be steadfast.

I confront death more calmly than I would have expected, sinner that I am. Life without Taijé has lost its savour. And I have lived longer than almost any others in our party from Geneva. I think of poor André, lost in the river torrent; of Pierre Bourdon and Matthieu Verneuil, drowned by Villegagnon; and of Oyster John and the others, meeting death at sea. We have had too much of water.

I would wish only that my ministry among these savages had led to a more secure planting of Christianity in Brazil. The first steps have been taken and I pray that others may arrive to build upon them. If so, let them take these monthly reports for a witness. The nearest approach to a Christian life has been within my own family in the palace (disregarding as *de necessitate* the sin of fornication, unavoidable for a man with nineteen wives above the Christian allowance). My love for Taijé, as hers for me, was surely blessed by You.

My children are the legacy I am proud of. They are: beloved above all, Rachel and Isaac; then my sons Samson, Jonah, Job, Jeremiah, Elijah, Isaiah, Zedekiah, Zebedee, David, Solomon, Saul; and my daughters Rebecca, Abigail, Ruth, Sarah, Naomi, Michal, Micah, Susanna, Hammoleketh, Judith, Leah. [Jacques misremembers the sex of the prophet Micah, and I can find nowhere in the Old Testament the improbable-sounding Hammoleketh.]

Into Your hands, Lord, I deliver them.

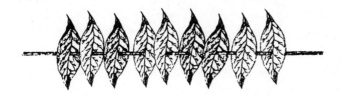

[The *Monthly Reports* end, therefore, with the certainty of Jacques's death and the strong probability of Friar John's. Beyond that we know nothing of what became of this remote mountain tribe.

As to the Europeans in the story, Jacques was wrong in his repeated assertion that there was no chance of Oyster John and the others reaching France in the worm-eaten *Jacques*. Their journey was indeed a hard one, several people dying of starvation in the later stages. Oyster John, or more properly Jean de Léry, gives a harrowing account of their troubles in his book *Histoire d'un voyage fait en la terre du Brésil*. What struck him as the most painful necessity in the crisis was the eating of the parrots which they were bringing back, each of them somebody's pet, tame and friendly, capable of limited conversation, and certain to be a source of admiring comment or much needed funds in France or Geneva. Jean kept his own bird hidden while the others fell in turn to the cook, but eventually he too succumbed. The skinny creature, consumed down to the least appetising morsels (he lists guts, claws and beak as the last to go), was sufficient to keep him and his closest friends alive for two or three days. He adds poignantly: 'I regretted his death even more when five days after I killed him we sighted land. This kind of bird needs nothing to drink, and it would have taken no more than three small nuts to keep him alive for that time.'

Jean de Léry reached Geneva early in 1559 and in May of that year he married. (This was the very month in which Jacques was making his difficult journey up the river; he was always too sanguine about his luck being greater than that of his colleagues.) By 1560 Jean had completed his theological studies and was ordained a minister of the reformed faith. He did not publish his book until 1577, provoked into doing so by the appearance of Catholic histories which his party considered, with some justification, to be over-lenient towards Villegagnon and unjust to the small group from Geneva.

On the day that Jean de Léry was married in Geneva, the Chevalier de Villegagnon was somewhere in mid-Atlantic sailing back from Fort Coligny to France. He had on board fifty savages, whom he later distributed round the court in Paris, keeping only half a dozen for himself. It was his intention to return to Fort Coligny with reinforcements, but he never did so.

The Portuguese captured Fort Coligny in 1560, after a siege of twenty days. Many of the French were taken into slavery, but sufficient escaped in canoes to found a new settlement on the mainland shore of Guanabara Bay, protected by Indian tribes hostile to the Portuguese. Here, continually expecting rescue by Villegagnon, they survived until 1567, when they were finally over-whelmed.

So Jacques was correct in his surmise, recorded in the *Monthly Report* of 3 November 1559, that there would be no safety for him in Brazil outside his own valley kingdom.]

APPENDIX

FROM THE EXTRACTS QUOTED by Jacques le Balleur it is easy to identify the ten pages of the 1556 Troyes edition of Rabelais which briefly became the Book of the Tupinili tribe. I append here the equivalent passages from Sir Thomas Urquhart's translation. The third book, from which this extract comes, was published after Urquhart's death, in 1693.

The sequence of the varieties of Cod is rarely consistent in editions of Rabelais, for it depends on whether the original columns have been read across or down by successive editors. Urquhart has needed some modification in this respect to tally with the Troyes version.

The Rabelaisian word translated by Urquhart as 'cod' is *couillon*. This literally means testicle, though the epithets chosen for it by Rabelais (with the change from thrusting energy in the first list to flaccid collapse in the second) make it plain that more is implied. Urquhart's equivalent was well chosen, for although 'cod' originally referred to the scrotum, it was used also in the plural for testicles. In the term 'codpiece' (technically no more than that part of a male costume designed to accommodate the cod), the word had come to be associated also with the male member: 'Why, what a ruthless thing is this in him, for the rebellion of a codpiece to take away the life of a man!' [Shakespeare, *Measure for Measure*, III, ii, 122].

The five leaves in question (pp. 135–44) are in the third of the four tiny volumes of the Troyes edition, running from early in chapter 26 to the middle of chapter 28. The marginal number of the lines bears no relation to that edition, being given here for ease of cross-reference with the *Monthly Reports*.

Thumping C.	Fly-flap C.	New-vamped C.
Bumping C.	Incarnative C.	Reverend C.
Tumbling C.	Brawny C.	Jogging C.
Berumpling C.	Hand-filling C.	Fine C.
5 Lechering C.	Satyrick C.	Fierce C.
Monachal C.	Formidable C.	Polished C.
Round-headed C.	Masculinating C.	Vigorous C.
Figging C.	Topsiturvying C.	Clashing C.
Spruce C.	Manly C.	Wagging C.
10 Plucking C.	Snorting C.	Tingling C.
Bouncing C.	Sparkling C.	Syndicated C.
Levelling C.	Superlative C.	Shooting C.

My Harcabuzing Cod, and Buttockstirring Ballock, Fryar
John, my Friend: I do carry a singular respect unto thee, and
15 honour thee with all my Heart, thy Counsel I hold for a choice
and delicate Morsel, therefore have I reserved it for the last
Bit. Give me thy Advice freely, I beseech thee; should I marry
or no? Fryar John very merrily, and with a sprightly chearful-
ness made this Answer to him: Marry, in the Devil's Name,
20 Why not: What the Devil else shouldst do but marry? Take
thee a Wife, and furbish her Harnish to some tune: Swinge her
Skin-coat, as if thou wert beating on Stock-fish, and let the
repercussion of thy Clapper from her resounding Metal, make
a Noise, as if a Double Peal of Chiming-Bells were hung at the
25 Cremasters of thy Ballocks. As I say Marry, so do I understand, that thou shouldst fall to work as speedily as may be:
yea, my meaning is, that thou oughtest to be so quick and
forward therein, as on this same very day, before Sunset, to
cause, proclaim thy Banes of Matrimony, and make provision
30 of Bedsteads. By the Blood of a Hog's-pudding, till when
wouldst thou delay the acting of a Husband's part? Dost thou
not know, and is it not daily told unto thee, that the end of the
World approacheth? We are nearer it by three Poles, and half a

172

Fathom, than we were two days ago. The Antichrist is already
born, at least it is so reported by many: the truth is, that 35
hitherto the effects of his wrath have not reached further than
to the scratching of his Nurse and Governesses: his Nails are
not sharp enough as yet, not have his Claws attained to their
full growth: he is little.

    Crescat; Nos qui vivimus, multiplicemur. It is written so, and it 40
is holy stuff, I warrant you: The truth whereof is like to last as
long as a Sack of Corn may be had for a Penny, and a Punction
of pure Wine for Threepence. Would thou be content to be
found with thy Genitories full in the Day of Judgement? *Dum
veneris judicari.* Thou hast (quoth Panurge) a right, clear, and 45
neat Spirit, Fryar John, my Metropolitan Cod; thou speakest
in very deed pertinently, and to purpose: That belike was the
reason which moved Leander of Abydos in Asia, whilst he
was swimming through the Hellespontick Sea, to make a Visit
to his Sweetheart Hero of Sestus in Europe, to pray unto 50
Neptune, and all the other Marine Gods, thus:

       Now, whilst I go, have pity on me,
       And at my back returning drown me.

He was loath, it seems, to die with his Cods overgorged: He
was to be commended, therefore do I promise, that from 55
henceforth no Malefactor shall by Justice be executed within
my Jurisdiction who shall not, for a day or two at least before,
be permitted to culbut, and foraminate, Onocrotal-wise, that
there remain not in all his vessels, to write a great Greek Y:
such a precious thing should not be foolishly cast away; he will 60
perhaps therewith beget a Male, and so depart the more
contentedly out of this Life, that he shall have left behind him
one for one.

CHAP. XXVII

How Fryar JOHN merrily, and sportingly counselleth PANURGE.

By Saint Rigomer (quoth Fryar John) I do advise thee to
65 nothing, (my dear Friend Panurge) which I would not do
myself, were I in thy place: only have a special care, and take
good heed thou soulder well together the Joynts of the double
backed and two bellied Beast, and fortifie thy Nerves so
strongly, that there be no discontinuance in the Knocks of the
70 Venerian thwacking, else thou art lost, poor Soul: for if there
pass long intervals betwixt the Priapising Feats, and that thou
make an intermission of too large a time, that will befall thee,
which betides the Nurses, if they desist from giving suck to
children, they lose their Milk; and if continually thou do not
75 hold thy Aspersory Tool in exercise, and keep thy Mentul
going, thy Lactinician Nectar will be gone, and it will serve
thee only as a Pipe to piss out at, and thy Cods for a Wallet of
lesser value than a Beggars Scrip. This is a certain truth I tell
thee, Friend, and doubt not of it; for my self have seen the
80 sad experiment thereof in many, who cannot now do what
they would, because before they did not what they might
have done. *Ex desuetudine ammittuntur Privilegia.* Non-usage
oftentimes destroys ones Right, say the learned Doctors of the
Law: therefore, my Billy, entertain as well as possibly thou
85 canst, that Hypogastrian, lower sort of Troglodytick People,
that their chief pleasure may be placed in the case of sempiternal labouring. Give order that henceforth they live not like
idle Gentlemen, idle upon their Rents and Revenues, but that
they may work for their Livelyhood, by breaking ground
90 within the Paphian Trenches. Nay truly (answered Panurge)
Fryar John, my left Ballock, I will believe thee, for thou
dealest plain with me, and fallest down-right square upon the

business, without going about the Bush with frivolous circumstances, and unnecessary reservations. Thou with the
splendour of a piercing Wit, hast dissipated all the louring 95
Clouds of anxious Apprehensions and Suspicions, which did
intimidate and terrifie me; therefore the Heavens be pleased to
grant to thee, at all She-conflicts, a stiff-standing Fortune.
Well then, as thou hast said, so will I do, I will, in good Faith,
Marry; in that point there shall be no failing, I promise thee, 100
and shall have always by me pretty Girls clothed with the
Name of my Wives Waiting-Maids, that lying under thy
Wings, thou mayest be Night-Protector of their Sister-hood.

Let this serve for the first part of the Sermon. Hearken
(quoth Fryar John) to the Oracle of the Bells of Varenes; What 105
say they? I hear and understand them (quoth Panurge) their
Sound is by my Thirst, more uprightly fatidical, than that of
Jove's Great Kettles in Dodona. Hearken; *Take thee a Wife,*
take thee a Wife, and marry, marry, marry: for if thou marry, thou
shalt find good therein, herein, here in a Wife thou shalt find good; so 110
marry, marry. I will assure thee, that I shall be married, all the
Elements invite and prompt me to it: let this Word be to thee a
Brazen Wall, by diffidence not to be broken through. As for
the Second part of this our Doctrine: Thou seemest in some
measure to mistrust the readiness of my Paternity, in the 115
practising of my Placket-Racket within the Aphrodisian
Tennis-Court at all times fitting, as if the stiff God of Gardens
were not favourable to me. I pray thee, favour me so much as
to believe, that I still have him at a beck, attending always my
Commandments, docile, obedient, vigorous, and active in all 120
things, and every-where, and never stubborn or refractory to
my will or pleasure.

I need no more, but to let go the Reins, and slacken the
Leash, which is the Bellypoint, and when the Game is shewn
unto him, say, Hey, Jack, to thy Booty, he will not fail even 125
then to flesh himself upon his Prey, and tuzle it to some

purpose. Hereby you may perceive, although my future Wife were as unsatiable and gluttonous in her Voluptuousness, and the Delights of Venery, as ever was the Empress Messalina, or

130 yet the Marchioness in England; and I desire thee to give credit to it, that I lack not for what is requisite to overloy the Stomach of her Lust, but have wherewith aboundingly to please her.

I am not ignorant that Salomon said, who indeed of that

135 matter speaketh Clerk-like, and learnedly: as also how Aristotle after him declared for a truth, That for the greater part, the Lechery of a Woman is ravenous and unsatisfiable: nevertheless, let such as are my Friends, who read those passages, receive from me for a most real verity, that I for such a gill,

140 have a fit Jack; and that, if Womens things cannot be satiated, I have an Instrument indefatigable; and Implement as copious in the giving, as can in craving be their *Vade Mecums*. Do not here produce ancient Examples of the Paragons of Paillardise, and offer to match with my Testiculatory Ability, the Pria-

145 paean Prowess of the fabulous Fornicators, Hercules, Caesar, and Mahomet, who in his Alchoran doth vaunt, that in his Cods he had the vigour of Threescore Bully Ruffians: but let no zealous Christian trust the Rogue, the filthy ribald Rascal is a Lyar. Shall thou need to urge Authorities, or bring forth the

150 Instance of the Indian Prince, of whom Theophrastus, Plinius, and Athenaeus testifie, that with the help of a certain Herb, he was able, and had given frequent Experiments thereof, to toss his sinewy Piece of Generation, in the Act of Carnal Concupiscence, above Threescore and ten times in the space of Four

155 and twenty hours. Of that I believe nothing, the number is supposititious, and too prodigally foisted in: Give no Faith unto it, I beseech thee, but prithee trust me in this, and thy credulity therein shall not be wronged; for it is true, and *Probatum est*, that my Pionier of Nature, the sacred Ithyphal-

160 lian champion, is of all stiff-intruding Blades the primest:

176

Come hither my Ballockette, and hearken, Didst thou ever see
the Monk of Castres Cowl? when in any House it was laid
down, whether openly in view of all, or covertly out of the
sight of any, such was the ineffable Vertue thereof for excita-
ting and stirring up the people of both Sexes unto Lechery, 165
that the whole Inhabitants and Indwellers, not only of that,
but likeways of all the circumjacent places thereto, within
three Leagues around it, did suddenly enter into Rut, both
Beasts and Folks, Men and Women, even to the Dogs and
Hogs, Rats and Cats.   170

I swear to thee, that many times heretofore I have per-
ceived, and found in my Codpiece a certain kind of Energy, or
efficacious Vertue, much more irregular, and of a greater
Anomaly, than what I have related: I will only tell thee, that
once at the Representation of the Passion, which was acted at 175
Saint Mexents, I had no sooner entered within the Pit of the
Theater, but that forthwith, by the vertue and occult property
of it, on a sudden all that were there, both Players and
Spectators, did fall into such an exorbitant Temptation of
Lust, that there was not Angel, Man, Devil, or Deviless, upon 180
the place, who would not then have Bricollitched it with all
their Heart and Soul.

The Prompter forsook his Copy, the Devils issued out of
Hell, and carried along with them most of the pretty little
Girls that were there; yea, Lucifer got out of his Fetters; in a 185
word: Seeing the huge Disorder, I disparked my self forth of
that inclosed place, in imitation of Cato the Censor, who
perceiving by reason of his presence, the Floralian Festivals
out of order, withdrew himself.

CHAP. XXVIII

How Friar JOHN comforteth PANURGE in the
doubtful matter of cuckoldry.

190 I Understand thee well enough, said Friar John; but time
makes all things plain. The most durable Marbre or Porphyr is
subject to Old Age and Decay. Though for the present thou
possibly be not weary of the Exercise, yet is it like, I will hear
thee confess a few years hence, that thy Cods hang dangling
195 downwards for want of a better Truss. I see thee waxing a little
hoar-headed already; thy Beard by the Distinctions of grey,
white, tawny and black, hath to my thinking the resemblance
of a Map of the Terrestrial Globe, or Geographical Cart. Look
attentively upon, and take Inspection of what I shall show unto
200 thee. Behold there Asia, here are Tygris and Euphrates: Lo
there Africk; here is the Mountain of the Moon, yonder thou
mayest perceive the Fenny Marsh of Nilus. On this side lieth
Europe: dost thou not see the Abby of Theleme? This little
Tuft, which is altogether white, is the Hyperborean Hills. By
205 the thirst of my Throple, Friend, when Snow is on the Moun-
tains, I say the Head and the Chin, there is not then any
considerable Heat to be expected in the Valleys and Low-
Countries of the Codpiece. By the Kibes of thy Heels (quoth
Panurge) thou dost not understand the Topicks. When Snow
210 is on the tops of the Hills, Lightning, Thunder, Tempest,
Whirlwinds, Storms, Hurricanes, and all the Devils of Hell
rage in the Valleys. Wouldst thou see the experience thereof,
go to the Territory of the Swissers, and earnestly perpend with
thy self there the Situation of the Lake of Wendelberlick, about
215 four Leagues distant from Berne, on the Syon-side of the
Land. Thou twittest me with my Grey Hairs, yet considerest
not how I am of the Nature of Leeks, which with a white Head
carry a green, fresh, streight, and vigorous Tail.

178

The truth is nevertheless, (why should I deny it) that I now and then discern in my self some indicative Signs of Old Age. 220 Tell this, I prithee, to no body, but let it be kept very close and secret betwixt us two; for I find the Wine much sweeter now, more savoury to my taste, and unto my Palate of a better relish than formerly I was wont to do; and withal, besides mine accustomed manner, I have a more dreadful 225 Apprehension than I ever heretofore have had of lighting on bad Wine. Note and observe that this doth argue and portend I know not what of the West and Occident of my time, and signifieth that the South and Meridian of mine Age is past. But what then? My Gentle Companion, that doth but 230 betoken that I will hereafter drink so much the more. That is not, the Devil hale it, the thing that I fear; nor is there where my Shoo pinches. The thing that I doubt most, and have greatest reason to dread and suspect is, that through some long absence of our King Pantagruel (to whom I must needs 235 bear Company, should he go to all the Devils of Barathrum) my future Wife shall make me a Cuckold. This is, in truth, the long and the short on't: For I am by all those whom I have spoke to menac'd and threatned with a Horned Fortune; and all of them affirm, it is the Lot to which from Heaven I am 240 predestinated. Every one (answered Friar John) that would be a Cuckold, is not one: If it be thy Fate to be hereafter of the number of that Horned Cattle, then may I conclude with an *Ergo*, thy Wife will be beautiful, and *Ergo*, thou wilt be kindly used by her: Likewise with this *Ergo* thou shalt be blissed with 245 the fruition of many Friends and Well-willers: And finally with this other *Ergo* thou shalt be saved, and have a place in Paradise. These are Monachal Topicks and Maxims of the Cloyster: Thou mayst take more liberty to sin: Thou shalt be more at ease than ever: There will be never the less left for 250 thee, nothing diminished, but thy Goods shall increase notably: And if so be it was preordinated for thee, wouldst

179

thou be so impious as not to acquiesce in thy Destiny? Speak
thou jaded Cod,

255 Faded C.

Mouldy C.

Musty C.

Foundered C.

Distempered C.

260 Discouraged C.

Forlorn C.

Unsavoury C.

Seedless C.

Dangling C.

265 Senseless C.

Worm-eaten C.

Overtoiled C.

Crestfallen C.

Loose C.

Extenuated C.

Grim C.

Wasted C.

Unhinged C.

Scurfie C.

Putrefied C.

Overlechered C.

Puff-pasted C.

Beveraged C.

Enfeebled C.

Deteriorated C.

Flaggy C.

Scrubby C.

Drained C.

Lolling C.

Drenched C.

Rusty C.

Exhausted C.

Pacified C.

Botched C.

Perplexed C.

Blunted C.

Trepanned C.

Emasculated C.

Corked C.

Confused C.

Mangy C.

Supine C.

Worn out C.

Spent C.

POSTSCRIPT

The page proofs of this book were sent to Rio de Janeiro in the hope of a Brazilian edition. As a result I received a letter from a publisher's reader, Senhor Manuel Guevara, to whom I am greatly indebted for his swift response. There is just time before going to press to include here the relevant passage from his letter. Senhor Guevara writes:

> I was intrigued to read of Jacques le Balleur's habit of naming his children, in Calvinist fashion, after Old Testament characters. My sister has in her employment a native by the unusual name of Zebedee. He says that his father and his father's father had the same name, but he has no explanation for this other than its being a family tradition. He comes from the mountain region of Barbacena. It seems hard to believe that this Zebedee is not a distant echo of the brief dynasty of Jacques le Balleur.

It does indeed. A living trace of that legacy of which Jacques was most proud, even if during the intervening centuries the line of Zebedee has been diverted — often by syncretistic methods not entirely unlike Jacques's own idea of mission work — into what he himself rejected, much of the time, as the papistical heresy.